Hope you -

To our

Beatrie Lederman Dream

5/10/02

Thoughts and Memories

Beatrice Lockerman
1940
24 years old

Thoughts and Memories

A Collection of Writings

Beatrice Lockerman Bollam

VANTAGE PRESS
New York

Published by Vantage Press, Inc.
516 West 34th Street, New York, New York 10001

Manufactured in the United States of America
ISBN: 0-533-13999-6

Library of Congress Catalog Card No.: 01-130693

0 9 8 7 6 5 4 3 2 1

To my family for their undying faith and assistance in getting this material together. It is a potpourri of my life and thoughts—some are memories—some written on the spur of the moment. I have included letters and documents when they are relevant to the span of years into which I have divided the work. Some are brief thoughts thrown in as an extension of what I was doing or writing about at the time and may seem out of place. Much of it is spontaneous—forgive me if I have digressed.

The part about my Parkinson's was left out until last. During these last twenty-two years, I have tried to put that in the background and live as normally as possible, and to some extent I feel I have succeeded.

I want to thank my late sister Brilla's grandson, Jeffrey Fisher, for creating the illustrations throughout the book and on the front of the dust jacket. Jeff is a commercial artist who lives in Smithtown, Long Island.

Contents

Introduction

Dear Children:

Before time and age dull my memory I must tell you about Dad and me. . . .

Granny Bollam used to say to me quite often, "What a pity you and Owen haven't kept a diary." And it is. All mothers should keep one for their children to laugh and cry over when they are ready to launch their own little boats into the uncertainties of parenthood.

Early Beginnings

All stories must have a beginning. That must be the most difficult thing about writing, for I have been years trying to begin a story—one that is simple enough and that is familiar enough to me, but one that still seems to have no beginning and no ending.

When Elsa Minarik, my teaching colleague and now noted author of the "Little Bear" series of children's books, would ask questions about my childhood and I would begin to answer them, she would say, "How wonderful, how simply wonderful it must have been," and I would begin to think so myself. Though it wasn't—not really. But then again. . . .

"Write it down," she would suggest. Then perhaps Elsa would tell again of her girlhood yearnings, how she would walk miles to try to get out of the Bronx and find some open space, a bit of "country," quiet and beauty, of lean times, when there was only bread to eat and one walked long distances to save the five-cent fare. There are many kinds of poverty and many kinds of wealth, they say.

I can't remember my childhood in any kind of chronological order, not to any great degree of accuracy. Who can? Yet, there are some clear-cut memories: things like the smell of pear blossoms outside my bedroom window, or the pinkness of peach blossoms, or playing in the cotton house on a rainy day, or watching Mama pluck feathers from the geese, which had been driven in and shut up in Henry's stable.

Just mentioning Henry's stable reminds me of our mules. I reckon we had some of the smartest mules in Sampson County—two in particular were Tom and Henry. Tom was short, red, and *very* intelligent (don't let anybody tell you mules are dumb). When Mama rang the big dinner bell letting us know that it was time to eat, Tom would stop wherever he happened to be and refuse to go any farther until the trappings of work were removed. Then he could be led to the stables and fed. Another smart trick he could do was bring in logs from the forest to the saw mill, having been shown the way only once. Also, Tom used to make sure his companion mule, who was hitched to the wagon beside him, was doing his share of the pulling by nipping him in the neck. Evidently Tom didn't like the way I attempted to mount him one time, because he nipped me too! Both Tom and Henry could open the latch to the main gate and let all the other mules out. The problem there was that once out of the corral, the mules would trample down the crops in the fields. To lead them back to the corral, we lured them with corn, which was their favorite food. Within a few days, Tom and Henry would repeat the entire performance.

An educated mule

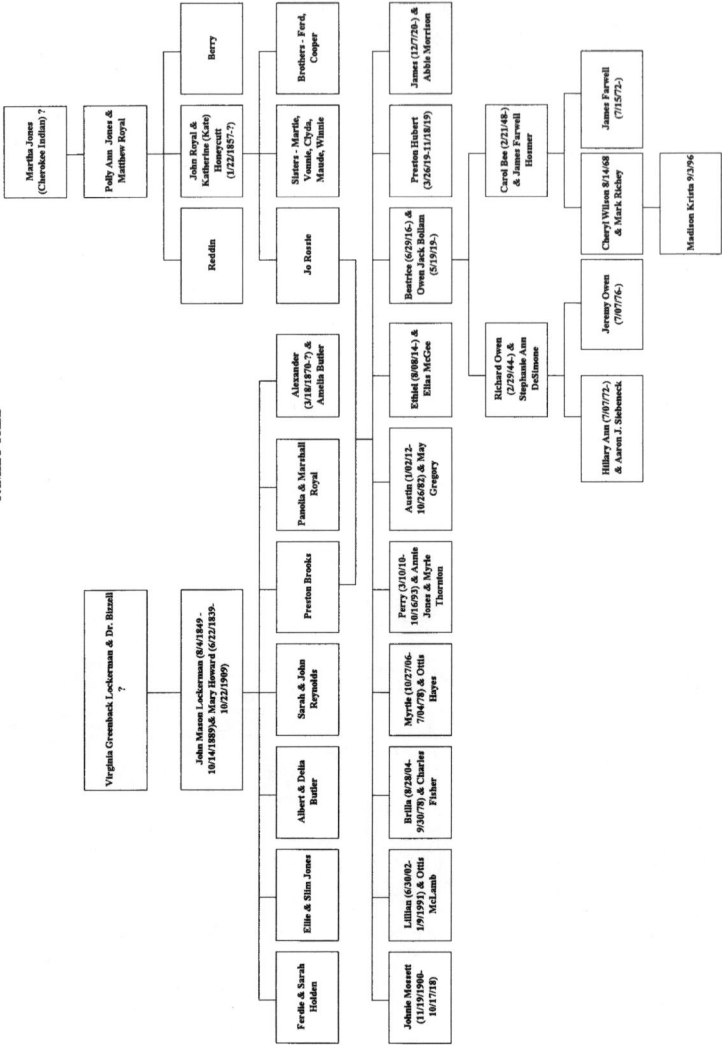

FAMILY TREE

```
Martha Jones
(Cherokee Indian) ?

Polly Ann Jones &
Matthew Royal

Reddin          John Royal &            Berry
                Katherine (Kate)
                Honeycutt
                (1/22/1857-?)

Jo Rossie       Sisters - Martie,       Brothers - Ford,
                Vennie, Clyda,          Cooper
                Maude, Winnie
```

```
Virginia Greenback Lockerman & Dr. Bizzell ?

John Mason Lockerman (8/4/1849 -
10/14/1889)& Mary Howard (6/22/1839-
10/22/1909)

Ferdie & Sarah    Ellie & Slim Jones    Albert & Della      Sarah & John     Preston Brooks    Panolia & Marshall    Alexander
Holden                                  Butler              Reynolds                           Royal                 (3/18/1878-?) &
                                                                                                                     Amelia Butler

Johnie Mossett    Lillian (6/30/02-     Brilla (8/28/04-    Myrtle (10/27/06-  Perry (3/10/10-   Austin (1/02/12-     Ethint (8/08/14-) &
(11/19/1900-      1/9/1191) & Ottis     9/30/78) & Charles  7/04/78) & Ottis   10/16/93) & Annie 10/26/82) & May      Ellza McGee
10/17/18)         McLamb                Fisher              Hayes              Jones & Myrtle    Gregory
                                                                               Thornton

                                                                                                  Beatrice (6/29/16-)   James (12/7/20-) &
                                                                                                  & Owen Jack Bedlam    Abbie Morrison
                                                                                                  (5/19/19-)

                                                                                                  Preston Hubert
                                                                                                  (3/26/19-11/18/19)
```

```
Richard Owen          Carol Bea (2/21/48-)
(2/25/44-) &          & James Farwell
Stephanie Ann         Housner
DeSimone

Hillary Ann (7/07/72-)  Jeremy Owen      Cheryl Wilson 8/14/68    James Farwell
& Aaron J. Siebeneck    (7/07/76-)       & Mark Richey            (7/15/72-)

                                         Madison Kristn 9/3/96
```

Thoughts and Memories

I
The Farm

It is the 1920s and early 1930s of which I now write.

Follow the dirt road out of Salemberg, North Carolina, in a generally northern direction. A short distance out of town, you will pass Mr. Benson Holland's farm on the left. He and Miss Lessie (note: In the South at that time, the use of "Miss" and "Miz" both had reference to a married woman. "Miss" was used with the first name and "Miz" with the last name.) have twelve children, and one of them, Annie, is in my class and a good friend. Theirs is a family full of fun and laughter.

A mile or so farther along, you will come to Dr. Underwood's place, at which point you turn a sharp right, past Ed Norton's cotton gin, then a sharp left, and Mr. Pat Jones's house comes into view. His daughter, Annie, will become my sister-in-law. A little way past the Joneses, the road enters a wooded area and snakes its way through pines and oaks until it emerges at a crossroads. You continue straight along, fences on either side, the Holden farm on the right—the Holden fields had more May pops than I ever saw anywhere else, and we loved stepping on the large green pods to hear them "pop"— and the Murd Matthews farm on the left. These farms are very familiar, as some of us kids (when we could be

1

spared at home) used to work here to make a couple of dollars to spend at the county fair.

Another way we had of making money for the fair was picking wild blueberries and huckleberries in the woods and selling them to the stores in Salemburg.

Suddenly you are alongside the big black walnut tree, around which the road curves to the right and slopes down toward another woodland and a little stream, which is the property line between Murd's farm and ours. One side or the other keeps trying to change the course of the stream to its own advantage.

Just past the bridge, on the left, is one of Papa's sawmills, and there is the huge house-high pile of sawdust. We spend many a happy hour climbing up and sliding down that sawdust pile! And just there to one side, shaded by oak trees, is the one-room house where Roosevelt and Bantie live. Roosevelt has twenty-one brothers and sisters, all by the same mother, and he sings all the time. Bantie is more serious, very quiet. I don't really know anything about her family. She and Roosevelt never had any children.

Perhaps one hundred feet beyond Roosevelt's house, the road bears left and begins to slightly incline upward, fences on either side. Albert McLamb's farm is on the right, ours on the left. About halfway to the house is a small fenced-in family graveyard. Only one tombstone stands there so far, for Preston Hubert, Mama's infant son (ninth child). Beyond that, another cotton field, and then Mama's garden, from strawberries to sage. Between the garden and the yard, a row of pear trees: luscious, juicy, eating pears and small, hard, pickling pears.

The driveway curves gently into the yard, a low hedge on the left, then a rock wall, built by my sister Myrtle, along the perimeter of the giant white oak that shades our front porch in summer and whose bare branches rattle in the winter winds along with the window panes in the front bedroom where I sleep. On the south side of the house are two chinaberry trees (the old timers pronounce it "chainy" berry) providing superb shade and producing sweet-smelling flowers in summer. A couple of sweet shrub bushes and a profusion of honeysuckle on the garden fence all combine to make the air heavy with perfume, a scent never to be forgotten.

Also on the south side of the house is a deep well where water is drawn to wash clothes in the wash house nearby, to drink on a hot summer day, or sometimes to use in the kitchen when the pump in the house runs dry or freezes up. This well is also used to cool the milk, which is let down in the oaken bucket to sit half submerged in the water.

The wash house, the smoke house (where meat is stored and cured), and a flower pit (where Myrtle keeps plants in winter) are separated from the house by a tall privet hedge. The wash house is the center of most of the activity. Inside is a huge cast-iron cauldron built into a brick furnace, so that a fire, fueled by wood, can be built underneath. In the cauldron clothes are boiled on wash day (soap is made when needed), and on hog-killing days it is thoroughly cleaned and used for rendering lard. Near the cauldron, on low benches, are the large, tin, rinsing tubs, the same kind we use in the house for taking baths.

To complete the tour of the area adjacent to that side of the house, nearing the southwest corner, stand an old apple tree and a couple of fig trees. Back to the front, to your right, running along the north side of the house, is the main "yard," large enough for two dozen kids to play games or several cars to park. This yard and the one behind the house are swept clean every so often with a yard broom made from reeds. To suit Myrtle, the broom's imprint has to be left in the light sand like wavy hair.

The yard extends to become a woodpile, and though Myrtle eventually tries to tidy it up with flowers and shrubs, it always looks messy. To the right is a large woodshed, and a hundred feet beyond that a building that was constructed with the idea of its becoming a filling station and store. But the Depression hit, and henceforth it is used as a packing house. On rainy days my sisters and I sit with a low bench in front of us, upon which we lay little piles of tobacco leaves, then gather them up, even the ends and wrap a single soft leaf around them two to three inches wide. Sometimes we work by lamplight if there has been no rainy spell and we have been too busy in the fields.

Running east to west from the wood shed to the wagon shed is one side of a rather large chicken yard, about an acre, I should think. The back quarter or so is wooded, and near the woods, inside the chicken yard, are two grape arbors, one black, and one white, the sweetest and juiciest grapes you could ever eat. Near the grape arbors are the sweet potato "hills," small straw-covered teepees.

At the left end of that side of the chicken yard is the wagon shed; and at the east end of the wagon shed, attached, but separated by a wall from the wagons, is the garage. Before the Great Depression, we had a number of cars: I remember a Model-T and a Whippet (my sisters Brilla and Myrtle even remember our 'Surrey-with-a-fringe-on-top'. Now we've given up our Dodge touring car and have to rely on mules that are used with both buggy and wagon.

The wagon shed can accommodate perhaps four wagons; but there are a thousand odds and ends stashed on

4

the walls, leaning against the walls and lying on the rafters above: kegs of used nails that Papa picks up at auctions, broken wagon wheels and harnesses, and various lengths of lumber, to name a few.

The chicken yard gate lies between the northwest corner of the wagon shed and the chicken house. The chicken house is set back from the shed, somewhat, and is large enough for a big family. My father never stints on lumber. Timber is cheap and he has mules to do the logging and two sawmills to cut up the logs. But he really does overdo it with the chicken house, though we do perhaps have a hundred chickens at any given time. It takes a lot of eggs and fryers to feed such a large family. In the spring and summer there are always wooden boxes filled with straw in the corners where "setting" hens sit on the twelve to fifteen eggs to hatch baby chicks to replenish the flocks. Mama dips her thumb in ink and marks the eggs that are to hatch so that if some laying hen muscles in on the nest, she knows which one is the fresh egg. Sometimes a hen will break out of the chicken yard and try to build a nest in some place hard to find, like under the crib at the far side and my sister Ethiel and I being the smallest are sent to fetch the eggs. It isn't unusual to be met by a snake because they like eggs too. When that happened it was the one time when I wouldn't be called slow, and I wouldn't even take time to introduce myself to that snake!

Farther back still from the house and reached by means of a path that runs along the west side of the chicken yard is the "john," inside of which is a long seat with three diamond-shaped holes cut in it, and always the inevitable Sears catalog. It is awfully cold out there in the wintertime, especially if there is a north wind blowing, and you can be sure there is no dilly-dallying. But, in

No dilly-dallying

the summertime, you can take time to browse through the catalog.

I have covered the buildings that are in the vicinity of the house, and I will now walk down the road that runs through the middle of the farm from the back of the house to the pastures and woodland at the western extremity. I walk slowly—I am a dreamer and a dawdler—and wiggle my bare toes in the sand. There on my right is the beginning of an orchard that was planted haphazardly in the fields, behind the stables and corn crib and then along the road until the next building and corral, which sometimes houses cows and sometimes mules.

But, now to the orchard. . . . Nearest the house are the peach trees. We kids can't wait until they are ripe to begin eating them. They look so red and so beautiful, but are oh, so green and bitter when we bite into them, that we throw them into the hedge. The apple trees around the stables are very large and bear very small hard apples, used exclusively for cider making. Behind these, in the field, are several other apple trees, including one that bears a yellow-skinned transparent apple and one we call "June" apple (red and very much like a Delicious). There is also a huge tree that bears what we call "Winter" apples because Papa packs them in sand in a large barrel for winter use.

The stables mentioned previously accommodate five mules. These open onto a corral, inside of which is a well and trough, where the mules have a constant supply of fresh, cool water. Above the stables themselves is a large loft where the fodder is kept for feeding the animals.

Farther from the house, but quite near the stables, is a corn crib, which consisted of three sections. The large middle section is used for the dry corn, which is so vital for food for all the animals on the farm. Family members

7

use corn meal as a primary staple and chickens use cracked corn. The end partitions of this building are also used: one for unginned cotton and the other for cotton seeds. In these two we play on rainy days, climbing to the back where the cotton is piled almost to the loft, and we tumble or roll down the soft cotton to the door. We make play houses in the seeds, for they can be paddled into shapes of chairs or beds or tables, or whatever we like. Once I got a seed up my nose and had to go to the doctor to get it out. In fact, that's one of the only times I remember going *to* the doctor. Once the doctor came to me when I had a high fever.

Perhaps one hundred feet beyond the corn crib, still on the north side of the road, is another crib, used as an overflow from the main crib, I suppose. But attached to this one are three more stables, for the cows, and another corral (or "lot" as we call it). Sometimes a cantankerous mule, usually Henry, has to be separated from the others and isolated in one of these stables until he behaves himself.

Beyond this building there are no other buildings except the dwelling of Ras and Mary B. Monk who served us well and loyally for many years. Their home became so ramshackle that they were forced to move out and go live on Prone Holden's farm. For a while this old house was used for storage—mostly fodder—until recently when it mysteriously burned down one night and Papa collected $500 insurance on it.

It was on this farm that I was born on June 29, 1916.

*   *   *

I'll start at the beginning. Except I do not know where the beginning was, or is. Perhaps in the Highlands of Scotland or the dance halls of Germany, depending on which story you believe regarding where John Mason Lockerman came from.

Perry got his information from old Henry Monk. And I expect old Henry had it straight. Old Henry's mother was taken away by the Yankees when Henry was an infant, and he was breast-fed by a white woman. Papa was born about the same time and in childhood formed a friendship with Henry that would last a lifetime. (Henry's wife, Sis, was a midwife who helped deliver Mama's babies. She and Henry lived on a ten-acre farm that Papa owned on the other side of Albert McLamb's place.)

Henry told Perry once (when they were taking a wagon load of cotton to the gin) that our granddaddy, John Mason Lockerman, was in fact the son of a Dr. Bizzell and a German girl who had been a dancer in Germany. Dr. Bizzell had gone over there for some reason or other, met her, fallen in love with her, and brought her back to America.

Being a respectable married man, he could not acknowledge her, so he quietly established her in a small house over in another township. When the child was born, she gave him her name—Lockerman.

Another version told me by another branch of the Lockerman family was that John Mason Lockerman came from Scotland as a young lad, landing at Holden's Beach, down below Wilmington, North Carolina. His intention was to go out West to settle down, but he got only as far as Sampson County (perhaps Duplin County at that time) where he bought a farm near Zoar Church, married Mary Howard, and settled down there in the community called Huntley about four miles north of Salemburg. The farm is still owned by a member of the Lockerman family.

9

Yet another source has a John Mason appearing in notoriously inaccurate Army records as being born in England.

John Mason Lockerman and Mary had at least seven children; Ferdie, Albert, Ellie, Sarah, Panolia, Alexander, and Preston Brooks, the last being my father. There may have been others who died as children, as it was rare for all children to reach adulthood in the large families of those days.

I know little else about my paternal grandfather except that he fought in the Civil War and lost an arm at Fort Fisher. He was a Justice of the Peace at one time as records show that "on 6 March, 1872 John H. Crumpler and Janette Matthews were married by Justice of the Peace J. M. Lockerman." (*The Heritage of Sampson County North Carolina 1794–1894 Ct. Historical Society*)

When war veterans returned after the war, the government gave them 'easy' positions. Grandfather was postmaster of Huntley post office from July 1877 until June 1893. Two or three times a week, he walked some twelve miles to Clinton to pick up and deliver the mail. The story was told that someone once approached him in a horse and buggy and asked, "Mr. Lockerman, would you like a ride?" "No, thank you," he replied, "I'm in a hurry."

Grandfather taught his children reading, writing, and arithmetic, which they otherwise would not have had during the terrible upheaval following the Civil War. I've heard it said that my father attended school only fourteen days. John Mason Lockerman died in 1899, and his wife, Mary, died in 1909.

"Pa John," as we called my mother's father, was the son of Matthew Royal and Polly Ann Jones. Polly Ann's mother was Martha Jones, a full-blooded Cherokee Indian. Matthew Royal was most likely killed in the Civil

War, and Polly Ann later married Dick Fann. They had four children—three sons . . . Carney, Lonnie, and Radford (whom people called "Rat"), and one daughter, Eelin. The three Fann boys were a wild lot and known far and wide for their uncontrollable tempers and readiness to get into a fight.

Grandpa John married Kate Honeycutt. I barely remember him, but I can recall many nights spent with cousin Eva Kate, who lived with Grandma after Grandpa died.

When Grandma Kate was about twelve, her father left to fight in the war, leaving Great-Grandma Beadie with three children: Berry, Reddin, and Kate. Months passed with no word from Great-Grandpa. Reddin, sixteen at the time, lied about his age in order to join the Confederate Army with the hope of finding his father. He never did. Great-Grandpa had been injured in battle and had been transported home in a wagon where he soon died. It is even possible that Reddin and he passed each other on the road. Reddin did not return home himself until after the war, when he learned of his father's death. (It was told that at the end of the war Kate had a dream one night that Reddin came home with a feather in his hat, and the next day, he did indeed come back, unscathed and wearing a yellow hat with a feather in it.) Uncle Reddin was still around with his long flowing beard, his fiery spirit and his tales of the Civil War until about 1940, when he died.

When Reddin left home, a great responsibility fell upon Kate's shoulders (reportedly about twelve at the time). There were no men left to plow the fields, so she did it on their farm and for some of the neighbors. I recall hearing her tell of hiding all the mules deep in the woods when the Yankees came through, taking or destroying everything in their path. However, according to printed records, she was born in 1857 which would make the circumstances even more remarkable.

I have a faint recollection of Great Uncle Reddin (Kate's brother) with fiery eyes and a full red beard. He married three times, I believe, and had a slew of children; but I recall only two daughters, Hortense and Calypso. Both were well-educated and accomplished pianists. When they came to visit us, I stood in awe of this accomplishment, their lovely white hands, and their manners.

Pa John and Grandma Kate had eight children who reached adulthood. I believe there were twins who died early in life. Jo Rossie (Mama) was the oldest, born February 8, 1882—followed by Vonnie, Clyda, Mattie, Maude, Ferd, Cooper, and Winnie. I remember them all except Vonnie. Uncle 'Coop,' as we called him, was born blind and ever remained so. He was sent away to learn to tune and play the piano. This way he earned a living. He was never without his pipe and always had a joke to tell.

I don't know how or when my father met my mother, though it probably came about through a land sale that Papa made to Grandpa John. Although brought up during hard times when gunny-sacks were used for winter clothing and when it was not unheard of for Papa to run down a rabbit in his bare feet. Papa had, at an early age, begun purchasing parcels of farm land and he sold one of these farms to Pa John, who then built upon it the big house that I remember so well.

At this time Papa owned a house in Salemburg and owned a small farm just outside of town. But it was a sixty-acre farm about three miles north of town to which he took Mama as a bride. I judge their marriage to have taken place about 1897—she was fifteen and he was thirty-one.

Everybody's hero—Uncle Reddin

The original house that was on the farm contained three rooms, a large pantry, and front and back porches. I believe the windows were wooden and swung open upon heavy leather hinges. The front porch was later extended to become a large middle porch, which we called the piazza—the coolest place that we could find to prepare fruits and vegetables for canning in the summertime—and five more rooms, a hallway, and a long front porch were added. The new addition caught fire when half finished, but by means of a bucket brigade, the fire was extinguished before too much damage was done.

Of the happenings that went on during the twenty odd years that Mama was having those ten children, I know nothing, as I was the eighth, except what I heard from others. She said it became fashionable to have a doctor come to the house when a baby was born, but she couldn't tell the difference between what Sis Monk did and the doctor did. These are memories, of course, that rise up out of the mists of the past, not sharp and clear cut, but emerging and receding in succession, like ghosts—the ghosts I used to imagine inhabited the graveyard I passed on the way to school.

My sister Lillian remembers going to parties where she played the piano and Johnny Mossett the fiddle, Grandma Mary coming to visit, and Lillian not liking her because she was so bossy. She wouldn't let her and Johnny Mossett make a train out of Mama's new dining-room chairs. Lillian also remembers going to Clinton in a surrey (with a fringe on top), when the town had a fence around it to keep the animals out so the streets wouldn't get littered with dung.

But there are sharper, more real memories of events that could have taken place over a span of many years. . . . A family around a large dining room table, with Papa at the head in full control, and Mama seeing to everyone's needs, not sitting down to eat herself until everyone else had finished. Of quilting parties in that same dining room, where the women would come on a winter's day, quilt, eat dinner (lunch), quilt again, until the quilt top had been finished. Of doing our homework on the dining room table at night by the light of a kerosene lamp, while at the same time there would be a semi-circle of chairs around the fire. Sometimes neighbors would be there with Mama and Papa, and those of us not needing to do homework would be there, warming our feet and sometimes standing to warm our backsides.

Always, in the winter, there was a fire in the dining room fireplace. Papa got up at 4:00 A.M. (having gone to bed at 8:00 P.M.) and lit it. Then he would sit there alone for a while, never quite understanding how anyone could stay in bed after 4:00 A.M.! About 5:00 he would call Mama, who preferred sitting up late at night and sleeping late in the A.M. But duty called, so she got up, dressed, lit a lantern, and walked down the lane to the cow shed and milked the cow. Years later I reflected upon this—that *no one* ever learned to milk the cow so as to relieve her of this chore—not even in later years when her thumbs would swell around the nails so that it was excruciatingly painful.

After straining the milk, she would grind the coffee and then go into the cold pantry to make biscuits. By this time the kitchen stove would be hot, the sausage and rice cooking, and eggs ready to fry.

Mama was an excellent seamstress and made most of our clothes, using patterns she snipped out of newspapers after we'd tell her what we'd like. She made the sheets and pillow cases and designed the quilt tops to use up

15

scraps of leftover materials. It wasn't unusual to buy material by the bolt.

Another task, which was hers alone, was plucking the down feathers off the breasts of the geese. Some thirty or forty of these ornery creatures would be penned up in one of the stables. Mama would take her little chair and some feather-proof bags to the next-over stable. One goose at the time was caught and held in such a way (head under your arm, feet held with left hand) that the right hand was free to do the plucking. The goose would be struggling and squawking all the time. It wasn't a job for the squeamish or sissies! Miss Sulie Jones said she used to be black and blue when she finished plucking hers.

In this manner farm families were supplied with plenty of feathers for pillows and warm feather beds for the winter. Another thing about geese that one might not know is that the female, when she left her nest, would cover her eggs carefully with straw to protect them from predators. Mama liked to use these eggs for cooking because they were so large. I remember it would take me quite a while to find the hidden eggs.

A lot of food was needed to feed such a large family as ours. Most of it was produced on the farm; the cows, the chickens, and the pigs were the source of an abundance of milk, eggs, butter, and meat. Then there was a huge garden and an orchard that both supplied more than enough vegetables and fruits. And there would be a whole row of melons through one of the fields.

Corn was a staple for both the family and the animals, so many acres of it were grown. Most of it was left to dry on the stalks, then gathered into the cribs for winter use. Then the dry fodder was stripped off the stalks (this was always a job for the men), tied in bundles, and anchored on the top of a stalk to finish "curing." But it was bad business if it got wet, so if a thunder storm threatened, we were all quickly rounded up to gather in the fodder. I hated that job because it left one sweaty and itchy.

Papa was a successful businessman from 1900 to the Great Depression. Besides running two or three farms, he went into the lumber business; he had two saw mills and bought tracts of timber and logged it to the mills, where it was sawed and sold. His services as an "estimator" were sought by other farm owners in our and adjoining counties. He would walk through a tract of forest and tell you how many board feet you could expect from it.

He was interested in politics, daring to be a Republican, and work for the party at a time when Democrats held sway. He was also interested in the law, which certainly would have been his profession, had he been sufficiently educated. Most of the farmers in our neighborhood could not read and would always come to Papa for advice. They would also come to share a bottle of "corn likker" behind the barn.

With the Depression there came a time when white women had to get out in the fields and in the hot sun to help the men raise the crops. The farmers needed large families then, so they would have more workers. In the beginning of the Depression, it was the cotton crop that sustained them. But by the middle of hard times, it was tobacco that gave them a more viable money crop.

When the bottom fell out of the price of a bale of cotton, Papa, who had several bales, was expecting to get thirty-five cents a pound, but had to settle for five cents. The government then got the big idea that the farmers had ruined the market themselves by growing too much and the best idea was to request them to plow in a percentage of what was already planted, paying them of course then and in the future not planting as much, thus paying the farmers to let some of their land lie idle. This policy still holds today. And farmers know a good thing when they see one: precisely what my nephew, who owns a large farm, said when we passed a good sized plot of weeds: "There's my money crop—okay?"

Papa agreed with the government on the idea of crop reduction to raise prices, and he was asked to go around to the farmers in our neighborhood to persuade them to plow up their crops. Some of them thought it was sinful, and they would be punished by the Lord and therefore refused. Others refused simply because they thought it would lower their incomes even further and they simply didn't believe they could live on less: and they didn't trust the government.

But a surprising number of farmers did agree to give it a try.

I had entered a statewide speaking contest on cooperative marketing, so I knew a bit about how the system worked. Papa asked me to go along with him and do the paperwork. We went in the buggy with old Tom at the helm—not having a car. . . . At this point in the Depression, I didn't know how to drive one anyway!

One person we visited on our rounds was the Poison Ivy Lady. People came from far and wide to visit her when they got infected, and, as I was very allergic to it, I was a frequent visitor. Some said she boiled some kind of root that she found in the woods to make a jellylike substance she rubbed on the rash while muttering some indecipherable mumbo jumbo. Then she caked it with talcum powder. And sure enough, in a couple of days, it would start to get better.

Another farmer we visited was T. Knowles. We knew

what the answer would be there, but we went anyway. It was "no"—"no"—"no"! The government had no business interfering with our farms. Louetta, his wife, agreed with everything that he said.

Ethiel and I often visited the neighbors, sat on a bench on the front porch, and talked just like grown-ups, except we didn't dip snuff or chew tobacco. Once this same Louetta told us that her daughter, who had died recently, had come back the night before and rearranged everything on her dresser—the supernatural played quite a role in peoples' lives and Knowles was said to be one of the meanest men alive. He had a bunch of children who were put to work as soon as they could lift a hoe. When somebody needed punishing and this was as good a time as any, he would line up the whole family and whip everybody, including his wife.

One of my "must" remembrances has to do with the attitude of men toward drinking. I somehow had a childhood revulsion against the convention that a young fellow wasn't really a "man" until he could take a few snorts of hard "likker." It was after Johnny Mossett became a "man" in that manner that he and Papa, both a little drunk, would get into violent arguments. Lillian told me of once seeing Johnny M. raise a rifle and point it at Papa's head as he walked away. She knocked it out of his hand just as it fired.

I do not, of course, remember my oldest brother, Johnny Mossett. He had left home in 1918, went to Norfolk, Virginia, and got a job. After three days, he became a victim of the worldwide flu epidemic that killed hundreds of thousands. When Papa was notified of his death, he sent two men (one was Ed Gilmore) to bring the body home. The authorities told them he had been buried already and they would not allow him to be dug up. They never did recover the body. He was buried in Norfolk, VA.

My brother Perry was the elder of the two brothers left at the time of Johnny Mossett's death. Perry assumed responsibility for the farm and the family when our father became bedridden. In later years the local paper published the story of his life as follows:

March 5th, *The Sampson Independent:*

To Treat My Fellow Man As I Would Be Treated

Perry Lockerman is a man who assesses a situation keenly, perceives his role of responsibility therein, and moves into immediate action, leaving behind a notably good record of accomplishment.

"I was born on a farm near Honeycutt's township in March of 1910. I walked about two miles to a little two-room school building, known as the Corinth Grammar School, until I completed the seventh grade. Then, I started going to the Salemburg school until I was about to complete the ninth grade.

"My father's health had gone bad, and he had made a lot of bad investments during the war. The Depression had come along and he'd gotten to where he couldn't work.

"We were poor and all we had was the farm. So he started keeping my brother and me, who was just next to me, out of school, one day and one the next day, to farm, plow and run the farm.

"So I went to the bed to him one day and told him that we were not going to pass our grades if he kept us out every other day. It was impossible.

"And I never will forget the look on him. He didn't give me a quick answer. He looked at me and he studied it a few minutes, and he said, 'I've lost everything in the

20

world I've got, practically, except this little farm. It's all we've got—all the children and your mother and I—to live on.

" 'I don't have one dime to hire anybody and I'm lying here flat on my back and can't move.' "

"Well," said young Perry, "one of us should stay here every day and the other one should go to school regular and keep a passing grade."

Whereupon his father looked up and said, "Son, that is a decision that I can't make."

Realizing what his father meant, Perry said, "Well, you don't have to make it. I have just made it for you. I start tomorrow morning working, so my brother can go to school."

And he never went to school another day of his life. He stayed home for some years afterward until all his brothers and sisters finished high school and college, for those who would go.

Deciding he wanted to explore the country then, he went to Philadelphia and Long Island, New York, taking various jobs as he went.

"I worked on some construction work. I worked with the federal hospital and just what I could do," he recalls. A strapping lad of just under six feet and two-hundred pounds, he met no problems finding jobs.

"After about two years, I came back to help my father look after the farm, starting back farming. Later I married Annie Jones, who was a neighborhood girl from near Salemburg," continues Lockerman, "and I've been around the county ever since.

"Back around 1932 I began to take right much interest in politics, and I've been involved in it a little, off and on, ever since.

"In 1938 I came to Clinton to work with Sheriff C. C. Tart and I worked with him for two terms, until 1946, as Chief Deputy. Then, in 1946, I ran for the Sheriff's office and got elected. And in 1950 I ran again and was elected.

21

"In 1954 I did not run. I went into business. I had a small insurance business—heliac and electric welding, steel, irrigation equipment, tubing and motors—and I ran that place down there until this past December a year ago. I was looking forward all the time until the day when I could retire.

"This past December I sold my interest in the business to my silent partner, Liston Malpass. Then the only thing I was involved in—as you know, eight years ago I did go into the Courthouse again on the Board of County Commissioners and stayed there for two terms. I did not run this time—and I only had that and my two farms.

"I did retain my farm. I brought the children up on the farm that I was born and raised on and my wife has the farm that she was raised on. And we bought a portion of the farm joining that. We have always kept the farmland and I've operated it all these years.

"I'd gotten out of the Courthouse now and I was retired so we could travel—as much as we could afford. I had gotten rid of everything that I'd been operating with except the farm property and I was still connected with the Tobacco Board of Trade. I had been sales supervisor on this market for seventeen years."

Perry Lockerman and his wife, whom he affectionately calls "Pete," were looking forward to traveling in their new camping vehicle, after his years of active participation in community, business, and political affairs.

"Then, last Tuesday, I got a call from the governor's office," states Lockerman, "and was asked to serve on the Road Commissioner's job."

Governor Holshouser plans to reorganize the Highway Commission, lowering the number of Commissioners to at least fourteen and even fewer if possible. There is a possibility that Perry Lockerman will not serve after the six-month reorganization period. "Somebody's got to go off," he believes.

"I don't know how I'll like it. But I intend to do for the

Governor the best job that I possibly can in this six-month period. I will not ask to remain on the Board after that, but I would like for somebody from Sampson County to have it," comments this elder statesman.

Musing a bit, Perry feels that he has had some temperament obstacles to overcome in developing as he wished.

"I've realized all of my life that I've had a lot of weaknesses, a lot of places that I need to improve and correct. But, a few things I've tried to do is to be as fair as I can and to treat my fellow man as I would like to be treated. That's one of my goals.

"Another one is, I try to tell the truth or I tell nothing at all. Many years back, I made a resolution that if I couldn't say anything good about somebody, I just wouldn't say anything, period. I think that's something that everybody should think about a lot.

"I will admit that at times I'm a little 'ash and anger.' I haven't held to that principle as well as I would like. Not near as good—I haven't been exactly satisfied.

"Somebody would push me wrong, do me wrong at times and I would say something that I would be sorry of fifteen minutes later. I've always had a temper, and it's the hardest thing in the world to control. But I figure if I can control myself, I can do pretty good with everything else."

Blessed with an unfailing and hearty sense of humor, Perry Lockerman has obviously done more than he may think in stabilizing tense and angry situations in his sphere of endeavor.

Skilled in the practice of politics, he believes that "practically all people will vote for the man that they think is principally, morally and mentally, the best man for that position in the primary." But it's very hard to jump party in the fall of the year, he feels.

"Now, I think this is more or less with the older class of people. I do not think that that applies to the younger generation that's coming in to vote now. I think that they are going to vote for the man.

"I don't think that they're going to allow, from now on, any one party to stay in power for too long. They realize that a strong two-party system is good for the people."

Of his political career, Highway Commissioner Lockerman states, "I never have been afraid. You know, a lot of times I've had people who've been afraid of their own judgment to do the things they thought were right, for various political and popular reasons.

"Some few years ago, there was an issue that I wanted to get across and they agreed, they thought it was right. But they thought that it would not suit the people, that the people would crucify us for it.

"So I said, 'Get a stenographer down here, give me thirty minutes to frame my story, and I'll stand up and argue my point. Then, when the next election comes along, blame it all on me and I'll take all the blame.'

"But," he added, "if there's any credit, I'm gonna take some of that, too!" And Mr. Republican, himself, threw back his head and laughed a loud Lockerman laugh.

He has enjoyed his life.

*　　*　　*

It was during the year, 1918, on April 22, when my sister Lillian ran away to marry Otis McLamb. She was not quite sixteen, and Mama and Papa had done everything in their power to persuade her not to marry so young. Papa called her to the back porch, she told me later, and begged her not to marry, not that he was opposed to Otis, but that he wanted her to get an education first. She was at that time attending a boarding school, and Papa said he wanted her to go on to college. But she did not listen and was picked up at the school by Otis and two witnesses. They drove to Sunnyside Baptist Church in Cumberland County, where the minister stood by the car (they didn't get out) and married them.

Lillian then went home to pick up her clothes—or so she thought. Mama was so angry with her that she wouldn't let her into the house. Papa, being of a softer nature, would have let her in, but one didn't cross Mama when she was angry!

So, Otis and Lillian went to his home for their first night together, and she had to borrow a nightgown from her mother-in-law, Miss Nursis. The next morning, before daylight, Miss Nursis flung open the bedroom door and told them to get out of that bed—there was work to be done, and she'd have no creatures lying in bed until sun up. Her husband, Mr. Auxie B., was a meek little man who wouldn't say "boo" to a goose.

Needless to say, it didn't take long for disillusionment to set in for Lillian. She worked in the fields from dawn until dusk and in about two months became pregnant. Though she became quite ill from her pregnancy, Miss Nursis did not let up in her demands. Mama by this time had forgiven her to the point that she felt sorry for her. Lillian was told that she could come home to stay until her baby was born, or until she had a home of her own. Toward this end she went into the woods with Otis, and the two of them, using a cross-cut saw, sawed down long leaf pines, which were lugged to Papa's mill, sawed into boards, and eventually went into the building of a three-room house on a farm adjoining Mr. Auxie B's—Otis's father.

Over a period of about thirty years following their marriage, Lillian and Otis had thirteen children. Two died in infancy.

My sister Myrtle on the other hand was ashamed for people to know that she worked in the fields, since white women at one time did not do field work. Myrtle wore gloves with just the finger-tips cut out to keep her hands white. She especially did not want Eddie Peterson, her latest beau, to know she had to do field work. Eddie drove a gas truck and passed our house daily; you could hear his truck coming for two or three miles down the road. Myrtle would run and get down in the nearest ditch where she couldn't be seen from the road. My brother Austin would yell to Eddie just as he passed our field, "Eddie, if you want to see Myrtle, she's lying in that ditch over there."

Remembrances

I would awaken in a pre-dawn summer stillness before the first outburst of the mockingbird in the chinaberry tree. Ethiel, who shared my bed for as long as I remember, would be lying next to me, her arm sticky to the touch. The top sheet would be kicked off when we went to bed and the bottom sheet would be damp with sweat. Hoping it would be cooler outside, I would lean my head out, careful not to dislodge the stick that held up the bottom sash, Papa always got up before day. He would get the fire going in the kitchen stove, then call Mama. The cow was milked and the biscuits in the oven when Papa began his rounds, calling each one by name, starting with the boys. "Perry, get up. Austin . . . get up"—on down the line through all of us, and adding, "It's going on seven o'clock," which meant it was about 6:05.

Our breakfast was nearly always rice, sausage, fried eggs, hot biscuits and coffee. Sometimes it was ham instead of sausage. On tobacco barning days, I ate just as slowly as humanly possible, so I think my stomach must have thought I'd suddenly lost all my teeth, and I had to "gum" my food.

Ethiel's reaction was just the opposite. Her idea was that the sooner begun, the sooner finished.

Growing out of babyhood, which was pretty early in our family, tended toward 'pairing' according to age: Lillian and Johnny Mossett: Brilla and Myrtle: Perry and Austin: Ethiel and me: Hubert (had he lived) and James. James, as it turned out, was the loner—'the spoiled rotten baby.'

Someone asked me once if I thought I was spoiled? "Don't be silly" I answered: "How could the eighth child in a family of ten children possibly be spoiled?" So Ethiel and I usually worked together, passing handfuls of green tobacco leaves, which Raymond MacDowell then bound to a stick with string. These bundles were then hung in the tobacco barn to cure. When the barn was full of these, the furnace was lit and the temperature in the barn was raised to a sufficient degree to cure the tobacco. The cured tobacco was then taken to the packing house. Here it was graded, wrapped, and made ready for market. I disliked this job mainly because my sister Ethiel was such a fast worker. She was always ahead of me, putting pressure on me to "hurry up!" Come to think of it, though, we were under the shade of the big oak trees around the barn, whereas when chopping and picking cotton, we were in the hot sun.

My brother Perry and I were the ones who *really* hated picking cotton. Very often, as soon as we had enough cotton in our bags to sit on, we sat and rested under the shade of the biggest cotton stalk we could find. My sister Brilla was the fastest picker of all and could easily pick nearly five hundred pounds in one day. Several of the men tried to compete with her, but she always won out.

27

Cotton pickers used sacks made of burlap (made from the well-known guano bags) with a wide band stitched to the open end of the sack. The band went over the opposite shoulder from the sack. There were also large sheets made out of the same material. At the end of the day, the cotton that had been picked was dumped on large burlap sheets, weighed and then dumped in a wagon, and sent on its way to the cotton gin the following day. It returned to the farm in bales, which Papa later sold.

All this was before the Great Depression, of course, when cotton was king. But now cotton was king no more, and tobacco had taken over from cotton throughout the South as the primary source of monetary income for farmers (many of whom had gone bankrupt).

The cured tobacco was taken to one of the large tobacco auction warehouses and sold to tobacco companies throughout the nation. We kids considered it great fun to go to the market to hear the auctioneers. My brother Perry was later to became sales supervisor on the Tobacco Board of Trade, a position he held for seventeen years.

My brother James originally ran a general store and gas station in Hamberg in Sampson County, North Carolina, from 1944 to 1945. Hamberg was noted for its belief in "hants"—ghosts. It must have been during the war because the one pump was empty, as I recall it.

James had devoted one section of the store to a pool table to attract his clientele when they wanted to stay and chat. The only trouble was the floor was not level, and most of the balls wound up in the top right hand pocket. No one bothered to shim up the leg.

Every so often he would run a sale. An example would be "forty-eight cents each—two for $1.00"! The customers would laugh when they realized they had been rooked.

James had a salesman come once who wanted to sell him fifteen or twenty dozen balloons. "Why would I want them?" asked James. "Well," replied the salesman, "you can sell each one for one cent and make a lot of money!" So he ended up buying those balloons. He soon found out that about every third one had a small hole in it. A young boy bought a few and came back complaining about the holes. "Well, of course there are holes," James reasoned with him. "The balloons bust if you blow 'em up too much, so the holes are supposed to be there to let the air out slowly." The boy looked bewildered, but he walked out without further complaint. A few days later, he returned and said, "Mist James, gimme mo of them balloons . . . but this time I don't want the ones with them holes!"

Later, James ran a general store in Clinton, North Carolina. One day a small boy walked in and asked if he could use the air hose to pump up a bicycle tire. He was told to help himself. In a few minutes, he came rushing in and said, "Mist' James, you owes me a new bicycle tire!" "How do you figure that, Junior?" asked James. "Yo free air just bust one o mine," he replied in deadly earnest.

Neighbors

I might say that if you think Southerners have some funny names on their birth certificates, here are a few, spelled just as they sounded to me. Take Alease Crumpler for instance. She wasn't a neighbor, just a student at Corinth School. She lived over at Bear Skin where there was one store, and her daddy owned it, I believe. Anyway, she

29

wore some fancy pink and white bobbie socks to school, which made me think she had to be rich.

Another odd name was Prone Holden; he was a neighbor, a bachelor whose property joined ours at the corner where the black walnut tree stood. Prone would come to our house on a winter's evening. I remember him sitting in the chair by the window where there was a little hole broken in a pane. Prone would stuff the curtain into that hole to keep the cold wind from coming in. He ruined the curtain, but Mama said it would do no good replacing it because Prone would only do it again as he was so often visiting, courting one of my sisters. You always knew which one; he had given her a piece of jewelry to indicate her. After a while, when he'd had no response from that one, he would give the next oldest one a piece of jewelry. Needless to say, he gave up after Ethiel, and I never got anything.

Not only were some of the names funny, but the individuals themselves had some pretty unusual character quirks. Take for example Lorenzy Tew, who managed to get religion about once a year in between drunken bouts. One particular story I remember involved Lorenzy. We had made a swimming hole in the stream that ran through our pastures, but it wasn't as good as the one at the creek. One day, Ethiel and some of her girl friends, James and I decided to go to the creek for a swim. We left our house dressed in our bathing suits. To get to the swimming hole at the creek, we had to pass Lorenzy Tew's house. He objected strongly to our display of skin. After we dove into the water, Lorenzy appeared on the diving board stark naked and proceeded to jump in. There followed a melee of screaming and a frenzied dash down the road.

Another bachelor, Murd Matthews, was a neighbor

who visited often. One time he told my brother Austin that he had no luck with women. He thought he must be doing something wrong and wanted Austin's advice. My brother enjoyed playing tricks on his sisters. He told Murd that he was going about his courting the wrong way. He told him, "Women like men who treat them roughly. Take my sister, Myrtle, for example. Try this method out on her; go up behind her, put your arms around her breasts and feel them. Just see what happens." My sister Ethiel was in the kitchen when Murd tried this approach on Myrtle. Ethiel picked up a piece of stove wood and cracked him over the head with it. He ran out of the house with blood pouring from the gash in his head. As he passed Austin, Murd cried out, "IT DIDN'T WORK!"

Addie Honeycutt's sense of humor was known throughout the county. He appeared often in court as a witness. And when he did, almost everyone in the county went to court that day. Once, he appeared as a witness in a case that depended, to a large extent, on good eyesight. The lawyer thought to embarrass him by referring to his thick glasses. "Mr. Honeycutt," the lawyer asked, "I notice that you have on very thick glasses. Just how far can you see?" "Wa-al," Addie drawled, "I can see the moon and they tell me that's 252,000 miles away." The whole room burst into laughter . . . end of case!

A good friend of mine told me the story of a neighbor—a man who had just completed fifty years of marriage to a disagreeable nag. He was on his death bed and knew it, but he would let go a volley of curses at anyone who came near him. Finally someone got up the courage to say, "Aren't you afraid to lie there cussing with every breath when you know your time is short?" "You can't

31

"Let's run Press off."

scare me with hell, young feller. I've been living there for fifty years!" And old Tom let go another volley.

My brother James related the following tale. . . . Addie Honeycutt and my Papa (Preston) were drinking partners. One evening they were lying by the open fireplace on homemade quilts, having had a few shots of "corn likker," and had fallen asleep. Mama had to step over them on the way from the table to the stove. Addie, half awake, sat up. Mama said to him, "I tell you right now, I'm not going to put up with but one drunk in this house!" "I don't blame you," Addie said. "Let's run Press off."

Church

I remember the chicken wire nailed to tablelike frames, covered with white linen tablecloths upon which the farmers, their wives, and children would pile the enormous amounts of food they brought: chicken, baked and fried all kinds of ways, pork, vegetables, and delicious desserts: cakes and pies, etc., etc., etc. for sumptuous church dinners.

Then there were the box lunch picnics. The girls would pack lunches for two, wrap them up like a gift, and then they would be auctioned off at church to the highest bidder. Their boyfriends, who somehow recognized their sweetheart's box, would bid and make the highest offer. Once, two local boys who had made it to big league baseball, came home with pockets loaded with money and bought every one of the boxes at the church picnic. The other boys were not amused!

As children we went to the Sunday School at the Corinth Southern Baptist Church. Familiar Bible lessons were taught to us through the use of bright-colored cards, each of which illustrated a story. From these and from the support of our parents, we all learned our "Thou shalts" and "Thou shalt nots." As we got older, we either were baptized or perhaps chose to stop going to church. I did not join because I was not convinced that I was ready, but I continued to go.

Many of the teenagers would get baptized on a dare, not because they believed, and I couldn't accept that. I was baptized after I went to Berry College where church attendance and Bible study were mandatory.

I Remember

When Grandma Kate grew old (Grandpa John had been dead for some time), she would go around to her children's homes to "stay a while" with each. Her mind was a little "fuzzy." She would do things like put a piece of homemade soap in a big pot of vegetables cooking on the stove to season them instead of the hunk of pork that the cooks usually put in. We would all have a good laugh over it, and Grandma Kate would laugh too, not knowing what she was laughing at. My younger brother, James, who loved to play tricks on members of the family, had a strong ally in Grandma Kate. But he had no love for Grandpa John.

Once Pa John and Grandma Kate came to stay a few days while Mama made Grandma Kate some new dresses. Mama was busy with her sewing and asked James to bring in some stove wood. "Wait a minute," James replied and continued playing with his toys. Mama asked him again and again he said, "Wait a minute."

After he'd said it for the third time, Grandpa's anger

got the better of him. He picked up James by the hair of his head and dragged him to the woodshed, telling him, "The next time your mama tells you to do something, you do it!" "I never liked Pa John after that," James later told me.

My sister Lillian's husband, Otis, learned all about working at the saw mill and became Papa's top employee for many years. I also remember him, sitting with other members of the family playing a card game called Rook. It was raining, as I recall that scene, otherwise we would have been in the fields and Otis would have been working at the mill. So I believe he was fully accepted by all the family. After Lillian gave birth to her first baby, Alimena, she would often hitch up one of the mules to the buggy and come 'home' for a few days. We all loved Alimena, except perhaps I was a little jealous, being nearly the same age.

After Lillian had had five or six babies, one of my older sisters said she would be afraid to walk through the room where Otis hung his pants! Unfortunately, poor Otis had diabetes and didn't follow the doctor's orders. For about the last fifteen years of his life, he was blind and lost a leg. Lillian took care of him to the end. After Otis died she lived alone for a while, but then she decided she would be happier in a home where there were people. She had spent too busy a life to spend the rest of it alone. So she went into a home at Falcon, a town where she had been to many camp meetings. She was very religious, had been active in church, and had played the piano for the choir (which Otis directed). There were several of her old friends at the home, so she was happy there until she died at the ripe old age of 88.

I Remember

Only a handful of things stand out in my childhood memories. From my earliest recollections, I had three pet fears. Snakes, Gypsies, and the Yankees. It seems that some Gypsies stole a baby somewhere in the South once, and the rumor spread; consequently, all of us children were told, "If you see Gypsies coming, run for your lives," which we did when they occasionally came through our country roads in their covered wagons. But when the Gypsies ceased to come, that fear gradually disappeared.

One might think I was afraid of snakes because Mama was so terrified of them, but she was also terrified of thunderstorms, while I—I loved them and had to be practically torn from the rooftop after scampering up with the aid of a ladder when a thunderstorm brewed. I was fascinated by the boiling unpredictable nature of the cloud formations.

As for the fear of the Yankees, that haunted me until I went far enough in American history to learn that the Civil War was actually over and there was no danger of Sherman marching through North Carolina spreading destruction. Funny thing, there seems to have been so little talk of World War I that I was utterly unimpressed by it, but Grandpa (my paternal grandfather) lost an arm in the Civil War and other family members were involved in that war, so that had made a lasting impression on me.

I did not start to school when I was six because they felt I was not strong enough to walk the four miles each day. But came the fall of 1923, I entered Corinth School, dressed in my flannel undies, button shoes, black stockings, and "hood."

There is a tale about my sister Myrtle and her husband Ottis Hayes. . . .

They were out driving one day and as they approached a main highway Ottis, who had a crick in his neck and couldn't turn his head, asked Myrtle if there were any cars coming. She was slow in answering, and as he proceeded out on to the main highway, she said in her slow Southern drawl. "Nooo, I don't see any cars a-coming" . . . Ottis proceeds . . . "but there is a big truck coming."

My sister Brilla came to New York to work, as jobs were opening up there before they did in the South. She married a "local" boy from Smithtown, New York. When she brought him home for the first visit, Murd Matthews came over to see Brilla. He took her aside and said "Brilla, I hear you married a Yankee. Ain't you afraid he'll shoot you while you're asleep one night?"

II

Education and Careers

"School days, school days, dear old Golden Rule days. . . ."
Oh, those halcyon days of school and youth!

I always loved school. You always love the things you succeed at.

*   *   *

My first day in school! I remember the route, all two miles of it, because I walked it twice each day (Ethiel remembers going in a buggy) that I attended Corinth School (called by some, Butler School). Cross the main road, through the big mud hole, up the lane, bordered on the south by Albert McLamb's cotton field, also his black and white grape vines; and on the north by T. Knowles's woods. Past Albert's house, burned down several years ago, then through another lane, more cotton on the south, corn on the north. Then through the woods, mostly long leaf pine trees, past the cemetery, and down the road until we reached Geddie Butler's tenant house. There Milton and Callie Boykin lived with their numerous children. Most every morning, except extremely cold ones, we would see them sitting on the floor of the porch, eating their breakfast of rice and syrup, or biscuits and syrup, using syrup can lids for plates. None of them went to school.

At this juncture we kids, swollen to about fifteen in number by this time, had two routes to choose from. One by the road, where, after there'd been a rain, we had to pick our way through the woods to avoid the mud holes, and the other through Geddie Butler's farm, climbing fences and trampling down his crops.

I was seldom in sight of the schoolhouse when the big bell would go "clang, clang, clang!" In one desperate spurt of energy, I would run until I could see the big oak in front of the schoolhouse, then slow down to a feet-dragging walk again.

Sometimes my friend Letha would be with me, but mostly for the last half mile of the two-mile walk, I was alone, outdistanced by all the other "older" young ones. I was slow, and—they said—just plain lazy. Slow eating, slow walking, slow picking cotton, slow everything.

"Miss Jackson don't care if we're late," Letha would reassure me. So we dragged our feet up the steps onto the little porch and into the cloak room.

On one side of this little six by six anteroom were shelves upon which were an assortment of buckets, cans, and shoe boxes containing lunches, mostly cold collards, cold sweet potatoes, cold biscuits, and cold pork sausage. Lucky the youngsters who had a peanut butter and cracker sandwich. And lucky if somebody didn't come out under pretense of going to the backhouse and steal it.

That first school house *is* one of the things that stands out more vividly in my memory. It was torn down years ago, but I can still see it, a frame building (one step above the log cabin school) containing two big classrooms, two cloak rooms, and two little porches, beside which the "little room" pupils and the "big room" pupils lined up to march in when the bell rang each morning and after lunch hour.

There was no difference in the size of the two rooms. The "little room" was so called because it contained the "primer," first, second, and third grades. The "big room," which every ambitious "little roomer" aimed at, contained the fourth, fifth, sixth, and seventh. Separating these two rooms was a row of folding doors, so that for community events the doors were folded up so that there was one big room. The rooms were heated with a big pot-bellied stove fueled with wood. Sometimes the pipes running through the rooms would break and create a panic until they were put together.

So poor were we all in those early Depression days—the farmers were the first to feel the effects of it—that one of the children would be sent to crawl under the school room to look for pieces of chalk that might have fallen through the cracks of the floor. We had three books—a reader (mostly nursery rhymes—so well do I remember "Little Boy Blue" under the haystack fast asleep!), an arithmetic book, and a spelling book. That was it! No library—no shelves with other books to explore. Nothing. Yet somehow those teachers laid the foundation for further educational growth. There was no water inside the school. Outside, about halfway between the school and the church (for it was used by both) was a hand pump. At recess, the students stood on line if they wanted a drink, and everybody drank out of the same vessel, a dried gourd with a hole cut on its side.

There was an outdoor toilet, and only one student at the time was allowed out. This was accomplished by hanging a stick with a hole in the end, through which a string was run. This string went around the neck of the student, and any student found outside during school hours without this stick was whipped in the presence of all the other students. My sister Brilla was a teacher there briefly, and my sister Ethiel said she got the worst whipping in her life then for insisting she had to go to the toilet when another student was out. Brilla showed no favoritism and no mercy!

I believe I attended Corinth School but one year. Ethiel and I must have been awfully smart, because when she was in the third grade, the teacher would often let her take over the classes while another unusually bright first grader and I took turns combing her (the teacher's) hair. And when spring came, my friend Helen and I seldom bothered to come in after lunch hour, but we continued playing in the "play house" that we had built in the woods, or wandered around picking wild flowers.

The next year, I do not know for what reason, we were sent to the "big school" in the town, where there was also a high school. When we started to Salemburg, I was in the third grade, having skipped grade two. I was devoted to my teachers, worked hard, so I ran into no difficulty. That was when I established myself as top student, and I never let go of that position for the remainder of my elementary and high school years. And there I stood, giving the valedictory speech as a senior.

At this point I'd like to mention that in those days high school basketball was the only interscholastic sport available for both boys and girls. I was a lousy athlete, but they always put me on the second string so that I could have the chance to go with the team. I never played, however. After basketball games and sometimes on weekends, we would go to Riverview to dance to jukebox music. I liked to dance. However, it was at these unchaperoned outings that trouble sometimes occurred.

There was also square dancing at various homes, and

it was at one of these that my father revealed his sense of humor. He was dancing with Mama and nobody else. Mama's boyfriend was milling around outside with a few other fellows who had no partners and sent word in the house for Press Lockerman to "Come out here and I'll give him the whopping he needs." Papa responded, "Tell him I'm having such a good time in here I wouldn't go out there for three whoppings."

In my teen years, there was such a stigma attached to getting pregnant out of wedlock that we avoided any relationship that would put us in a position where getting pregnant was possible. Desires were suppressed. I'm not saying some did not yield, and some who did were lucky and didn't get "caught." Rarely, one did, and the assumption was that she was "ruined." But, if she got married quickly, her lack of discretion was more or less overlooked, but never forgotten. I'll wager my mother knew every woman in the county who had had a shotgun wedding, and woe betide one who tried to put on 'airs'!

I also liked music. I remember Papa had bought a piano for Lillian, but she left home to get married at the age of fifteen so did not have time to take music lessons. My brother Austin was the only one in the family who ever took lessons. I would take his music books and a kerosene lamp, and by its light, I learned the notes and signs. That was the beginning of my love of music. I remember Austin doing the leading part in an operetta called *Lord Jeffrey Amherst.* I became a member of a trio, the only musical group in our high school, I believe. Music wasn't stressed to any great extent. It was mostly good old "reading, 'riting and 'rithmatic." But they had a fairly well equipped library, and I took advantage of it.

High school days were the fun days of my life. I had several friends, and we "grew up" together. We began to cut the apron strings, but never completely, which is the way it should be. I remained very independent and refused to smoke just because everybody "did" it. I tried it and simply didn't like it.

We were four girls and one boy in our "gang." Elmer was, even then, interested in old people and went on to become a doctor, specializing in geriatrics. He was quiet and a little shy, so you can imagine how surprised the class was when he brought Miss Matthews (a no-nonsense history and French teacher) a present all wrapped up nicely and put it on her desk. When she opened it, out jumped a cute little mouse! She screamed and jumped on her desk. She was not amused, but the rest of the spectators were laughing their heads off. I forget what the punishment was. I expect it was "Go to the Principal's Office!"

Now our principal, Mr. Cusick, was as nice a man as you would ever want to meet—a real gentleman. But he punished the old-fashioned way. He controlled the library, which was near his office, just by looks. There was no teacher on duty; the taxpayers couldn't afford it. But if it got the least bit noisy, Mr. Cusick would come to the door and just stare. He didn't have say a word. You could hear a pin drop.

Mr. Cusick had another way of punishing the stronger boys. When the school house was built, it was new ground and there were a lot of stumps still left standing. Mr. Cusick devised a plan whereby students dug these stumps as punishment. It is said that my brother Austin and his buddy Glenn Newman (who also became a doctor) dug about ninety percent of those stumps for doing such things as nailing the rubbers of a teacher they didn't like to the floor on a rainy day or enticing a shy, unlikable girl

Elmer's present was a big surprise to Miss Matthews.

behind a door and feeling her breasts when all the students were supposed to be out for recess.

There were dances at the high school, well chaperoned, at which the girls carried "date" cards with numbers from one to ten, assuming she might be that popular. A "date" usually consisted of walking up and down the halls holding hands.

Things became desperate during my senior year. I had no financial backing at all from my parents due to the Depression, and I desperately wanted to go to college. Then I saw an ad in an agricultural paper about Berry College in Rome, Georgia, where one could go completely free by working one's way through. I answered it and was accepted on the condition that I paid the first $100. I was so excited that I believe I jumped every fence from the mailbox home. But where, oh where, could I get that $100? One of my teachers was quite well off and loaned me the $100 for the first term.

Being accepted at Berry College, where I could work my way to a degree, was the height of my ambition. I knew I didn't like farm work, and I figured the best way to get off the farm (the way it was during the Depression years, which was all I knew or remembered) was to go for a good education. By the way, only two others from my graduating class of 25 students went to a four-year college. I believe that was about par for the course.

Berry College is a wonderful institution where thousands of worthy students, who otherwise would not have been able to go to college, were able to get a college degree. When I went off to Berry, my sister Ethiel, who was two years older than I was and had graduated from high school, was still at home working and unhappy. She wrote me and asked me to try to get her in the college as a full-time working student during the second semester. I went to see the president of Berry College and was able to get her accepted.

All students had to work two days each week to pay for room and board. Tuition had to be paid for in cash or the student had to work full time for one semester to pay for a full year. By the way, I wasn't top student at Berry, but I did well enough to work the rest of the way through, and I graduated in 1939.

I Remember

On a hot, oppressively heavy afternoon of a September day that year, 1934, they took me, my little handbag and my big trunk to Dr. Sessom's house. His son, E.T., and I would be traveling together on the train to Rome, GA. E.T. had been attending Berry High School for boys, and I was entering Berry College as a freshman.

For me, this was a brand new experience, my first real break with home and family. My $100 tuition money was dutifully pinned inside my bra, and there was enough money for a one-way train ticket and a few incidentals in my pocketbook. That was it! From now on I would be on my own; I knew and understood that. But I had no qualms about what I was doing.

We were all night on the day coach of that dirty, old rickety train, with changes in Fayetteville, Florence, and Atlanta, and stops at a thousand little towns, with the diminishing chug-a-chug-a followed by bang-bang-bang-creak-stop! Few passengers got on, so we had plenty of room and could stretch our legs on the seat across from us. Between stops we leaned on each other and dozed. Occasionally E.T. would plant a gentle kiss on my cheeks or forehead that said only "Take courage, Little Bea; everything's going to be okay." He was like that—gentle, kind, with an easy laugh. We were always friends, but nothing more.

When we arrived at the Rome Station the next A.M. there were conveyances there both for us and our trunks. I was driven the few miles to the college through the "Gate of Opportunity," and eventually delivered to the entry-way of the Ford Quadrangle and told the office was on the right. Thus began what was, in a sense, five years of "military" training.

The first order of the day was to get measured for three uniforms. Normally, I never remember clothes (it is the face that sticks like a leech to my little memory box). But if you wear a uniform for five years, you're not likely to forget its general appearance. Underclassmen wore pink chambray dresses, long sleeves, fitted waistband, full skirt (the proper number of inches from the floor), and stiffly starched detachable white collar and cuffs. Seniors wore the same uniform in pastel green. There were black shoes and stockings for winter wear, white for summer wear, one black wool suit for church on Sunday in winter, and one white cotton dress for the same in summer. There was one dark blue raincoat, one dark sweater, one pair of rubbers, and one black umbrella. We were prepared; and there were no excuses, other than illness, for missing a single class or a meal (with the exception of Sunday breakfast) or Sunday school, or church, no matter what the weather.

Rules, rules, and more rules! Tardiness was not tolerated; everyone stood in the dining hall until a prayer was sung by the student body—I remember the Sunday one began "Safely through another week God has brought us on our way" (usually led by Cleo Garner). The food was fairly good, most of it produced by the college; plenty of

47

milk and butter, obtained from the college dairy. Students ran everything and did all the work. It was practically a self-sustaining little world, and beautifully kept, several thousand acres, including "Lavender Mountain."

It was during my first year at Berry College that I met and began dating Franklin Cotton. From that point on, I was considered his girl, and no other boy would ask me for a date, even though I would have preferred the company of other boys at times.

Dating at that time consisted of strolling around a well-chaperoned campus on a Sunday afternoon. There were dances in the evening, also well-chaperoned, with no close holding permitted. Holding hands was the limit of your contact at all times.

Regarding further education for the rest of the family, Lillian was married already, having been attending boarding school at the time of her marriage. Brilla and Myrtle, after finishing high school, went to Miss Waterhouse's Secretarial School, also part of Pineland Junior College in Salemburg. My sister Ethiel and I were the only ones to get a college degree. Papa would have been proud of us had he been living. Unfortunately he died in 1937.

I'd like to tell you a few things about my father, whom I don't remember when he was well, since I was near the end of the line. He was not an affectionate man, but he stood four-square behind us if we were in need. And though, even as a child, I abhorred his drinking, I had great respect for his knowledge and intelligence. I remember once, when I thought he was dying and we all stood around with long faces, out of the blue I said, "Smile, Papa."—I must have been about four at the time—and he smiled and everybody else broke out in a big laugh.

III

Romance and Marriage

The summer of 1941 had been a busy one for me. After school was out (it had been my second year of teaching at Baron DeKalb), we had taken off for New Orleans—Sally, Dora, Ethiel, and I. New Orleans had been picked for our school vacation because my friend Franklin, having volunteered for the Army after graduation, was stationed near there. Sally, ever the match-maker, was trying to propel me into matrimony.

The whole thing was a disaster. We could not sleep at night because of the heat; we all got blistered lying on the beach at Lake Pontchatrain; and I left New Orleans less sure than ever that I cared enough for Franklin to marry him.

Back home in North Carolina, I had two days to get things ready for summer school at the University of Tennessee, where I would take refresher courses in Business (Accounting, etc.), which I was to teach in the fall at Baron DeKalb High School in Westville, South Carolina.

While attending the University of Tennessee that summer, I responded to a notice in the paper regarding employment with the FBI. I discovered that the FBI had a recruiting office in Knoxville for those interested in applying for work in Washington, D.C., the results of which will appear later in these memoirs.

Jack gets his RAF wings.

A Preview

My mother said it would never last, this marriage of mine to a stranger, a foreigner (from England) whose courtship was by correspondence and whose engagement was by telegraph. But that was fifty-six years ago.

After I returned to my teaching job in Westville, South Carolina, in late August 1941, the first Sunday I was there, Arthur, whom I had dated the previous year, came out from Camden with a couple of British lads looking for dates for them. These lads had come from England to be trained as pilots as part of the Lend-Lease program. We went out several times as a group. Jack was dating Evans, but our fates were determined that first Sunday, and we knew it. He later told me that the very first time he saw me, he said to himself, *There's the girl I want to be the mother of my children.*

Jack continued his training in Macon, Georgia, and at this time our correspondence began. My roommate and I planned a weekend trip to Macon, and at last we were together.

Jack finished his training at Selma, Alabama, and Pensacola, Florida, where he received his wings.

In the meantime, while home for the Thanksgiving holidays, I received a telegram to report to the FBI in Washington on Monday A.M. It seemed we were destined never to meet again, for he would soon be flying home to England. I had not been on my new job long enough to have accumulated any days off, but I had a kind, understanding supervisor who gave me four days.

I took off as soon as I could pack, and Jack was in Birmingham to meet me. But it was with a sad heart that I returned to Washington not knowing if I would ever see him again. He would soon return to England to join his squadron.

Our daily correspondence continued, but tightly censored. Then one day I received a telegram, "Darling, I saw a beautiful ring. Would you accept it?" I wasted no time in responding, "Yes!"

As luck would have it, Jack was posted back to Canada, as an instructor and as soon as he could get enough time off, he came down to Washington. He was detached from the RAF on service pay, and all he had with him when he got there was my engagement ring. So I wound up paying for my wedding ring, hotel room, and honeymoon combined . . . and we were married in a little church nearby with a few friends and my sister Ethiel, in attendance. I always tease him by telling him he married me for my money.

Here I retrace my steps a little in order to fill in some of the details of our romance while still in the United States. I submitted this piece some few years ago.

Dear Canada
(submitted for publication at an earlier date)

In 1942, while employed in a government office in Washington, I met three Canadian girls and was so impressed by their friendliness and courtesy that I decided Canada must be a wonderful place. Little did I realize that in a few short weeks I would be on my way to Nova Scotia to become one of the many American wives of RAF and RCAF personnel who found the doors of Canadian homes opened to them during the war. It is because of this hospitality that I wish to send this expression of grat-

52

itude for the happiness that we American girls found there.

I was very tired when I reached Truro, having been on the train more hours than I could keep track of.

It was 10:00 P.M. and the season's first snowflakes were falling. My husband (of four weeks standing) was at the station awaiting me, and in approximately five minutes, we were at Jean's front door. Dear Jean Boss greeted me with a hearty "Well, thank goodness you got here at last!" She had one of the most cheerful and good-natured faces I have ever seen, before or since. She spent all her spare time writing letters and making up parcels for the boys overseas or the service couples who had lived with her from time to time; or standing on the station platform with baskets of fruit and sandwiches to hand out when troop trains were passing through. Ira, her husband, worked on the police force and had a heart as big and generous as hers.

Our stay in Truro was short-lived, only about two months, but I have very vivid and pleasant memories of lovely walks in the snow, of a skating rink that we made in Jean and Ira's backyard, of the most delicious pies and cakes that Jean baked for us, and of all the jolly people we met in their home.

Our next move was to Charlottetown, PEI, where we went to live with "Janie." How I ever came to call her that I don't know, but perhaps our relationship was too close to say "Mrs." It was her name, of course, but she had four children who were as old or older than myself, so to some it may have seemed strange to hear me saying "Janie."

The year we spent on the Island was happy and carefree. I joined a church choir and women's group, where I felt at home from the very beginning, so hospitable were the women I met there. Soon I became friends with the girls in the grocery and department stores, and I chatted familiarly with people on the streets. In Charlottetown I also met Rose, from Michigan, and Doris, from Tennessee. There were other American girls whom I did not know so well, but these two still write of the happy times that we had.

Everybody made jokes about being isolated and cut off from the rest of the world, especially in winter when the ferry got stuck in the ice so frequently. When I went back to Truro to visit Jean, I decided to take the Wood Island Ferry, but when we got ready to "sail," there was so much indecision on the part of the boatmen because the sea was stormy, that I had visions of having to return to Charlottetown. After about two hours' delay, however, they decided that perhaps they could make it with luck, and lifted anchor! I must confess that I was full of misgivings and halfway out would have given almost anything to be safely on either side. The next time I left the Island, I chose the plane, which had always, I believe, given reliable and dependable service.

In January 1944, my husband was posted to Goderich, Ontario. My baby was due in about a month's time, and although the doctor assured me it was safe to travel, Janie would not hear of my going, as I knew no one in Goderich and we had no place to stay there. She insisted upon taking care of me during that last month, and I honestly do not believe my own mother could have done it with greater care or concern. On February 29, I gave birth to my first baby, a boy, on Canadian soil. The next day there arrived, by express, a bassinet, four nighties, and three hand- knitted sweaters for my baby from Jean. During my eight-day stay in the hospital, I received gifts daily from kind friends in Charlottetown. When I left the hospital, I went back to Janie's for another three weeks.

All this time she had refused to take any rent from me, saying that it was her gift to the baby, to say nothing of the fact that she was also boarding me!

My plane reservation was scheduled for the last Thursday in March. Jack had written that he had found what seemed an impossibility—a whole house, furnished, for forty dollars per month. It was with mixed feelings of sadness and enthusiasm that I packed my bag and bundled my four-week-old baby into a basket early that Thursday morning.

The little plane lifted us gently upwards, then settled down at a low altitude over the Island, Northumberland Strait, and very shortly arrived at Moncton. Complications arose. An unexpected storm was coming up from the States, extending almost all the way from Moncton to Montreal. Our plane was grounded. About an hour behind schedule, one did take off, but I was left behind upon the advice of the stewardess who thought it would be unwise to take the baby. However, arrangements were made to take me on the next plane to Montreal. A few minutes after the take-off, we were instructed to put on oxygen masks. The baby, being the last to have his adjusted, lost his 10:00 A.M. feeding. The stewardess took him over, held his mask, and he slept the rest of the way.

The storm offered no threat from Montreal to Toronto. I was fortunate in having beside me a man who showed me every kindness. Not only did he assist in changing the baby (explaining that he was the father of four, so knew all about it!), but he stayed with me at the Toronto Airport until I inquired about my train to Goderich. I had missed the last one and had to spend the night in Toronto, whereupon he insisted I take the room he had reserved for himself at the hotel.

Shortly after I arrived at our new home in Goderich,

the telephone rang. It was my next door neighbor, offering to help with the baby. She had one six months old so might be able to help me at times when I wouldn't know what to do. I soon became very good friends with Olive, her husband, Clare, and little son, Robert. They gave us part of their garden plot, so we could have a garden of our own that summer. And it was they who gave us a farewell dinner after another happy year in Canada, when at last we knew the end of our visit to your country had come. I returned to my home in North Carolina, and my husband went back to Nova Scotia for a short training period before flying back to England.

And so, to all the Jeans and Iras, the Janies, and the Olives and Clares throughout Canada, I wish to say Thanks again and to reiterate that we do not believe there exists anywhere on this earth a kinder, more generous people.

1939–1945

These years were the high point in my life—in retrospect, the happiest. On the surface that would appear paradoxical, as the first two years were spent under the clouds of an upcoming war, and the last four involved that war. But during this period, I left the sheltered, strictly chaperoned life of Berry College, went out into the Big World, and held my own—successfully held two jobs, widely different in their aspects; fell in love, married, and had my first child—all heady stuff!

At a time (Spring 1939) when jobs were very difficult to come by, I had a positive response to my first application. Perry, Annie, Mama, and James had come to my graduation and I had arranged to stop at Westville, South

Carolina (en route home to N.C.) for an interview for a teaching job. I had hoped to teach high school English, but the superintendent, Mr. Busbee, said he had a good English teacher. He needed a public school music teacher. Music was being added to the curriculum for the first time and he thought, having gone over my record, that I could handle it, provided I went to summer school for a couple of courses in music and education. I accepted his offer and signed the contract.

Problem: I had no clothes, no money, nothing. Since Papa's death and Perry's departure, the farm had been rented so there was no money there. I decided to try for summer work at the University of North Carolina and landed the job of collecting the laundry in my dorm. I did a column for the campus paper, but I don't believe I was paid for that. Myrtle was working, so I expect she paid for clothes, as I do remember going away with new clothes. A local school principal was also going to university, so I was able to go up with him, which saved me bus fare.

Some six months earlier, the armed Merchant Cruiser, HMS *Chitral,* sailed from Gorough, Scotland, not in convoy, for in those days of the war men who were to be trained under the Lend-Lease agreement were dispatched to their bases with the greatest possible speed.

Aboard the *Chitral* was a group of young eager fellows, mostly from England, on their way to be trained as pilots in the Army Air Corps. Of that voyage I shall let Dad tell you in his own words in two letters he wrote to Granny and Grand-dad at the time.

May 1941: A Letter Sent from Jack to His Parents

These are awfully awkward letters to compose since the contents are strictly confined by the censor and I don't want him to waste his precious blue pencil. Everything exciting will have to wait until I'm back home and I suppose they will have lost their colour in events to come.

It seems I've been on this boat for months, but although long enough it's nowhere near that long. It's been quite a pleasant time mostly, but a very idle time filled by reading and lying on deck. We had complete run of the ship except the boat deck and bridge and even the crows nest and engine room have been thoroughly explored. The crow's nest on a moonlight night is wonderful, so ethereal and detached from everything. Way above the ship, with an unbroken line of horizon with a silver path of moonlight clear to its edge. You wonder however you got that high at sea and whether you'll bother to ever come down again. It's a quiet sort of life at sea, one that detaches you from all things, even the dangers imagined so vividly on land. There's none of that anticipation for these dangers, one would have thought. They just don't belong in the blue sea and the sky and the little world of iron and wood.

We watched flying fish go skipping across the waves and phosphorescence in the foam around the bows. We've felt the ship go pitching and tossing and riding the Atlantic swell, and it's been calm and clear and the sea a wonderful cobalt blue, so deep and intense it's hard to believe; Prussian blue as it curls from the bow and melts into snowy, soft white foam and transparent blue green eddies disappear in the velvet tinted blue touched with rose from a setting sun. It's too wonderful to carry in memory and too beautiful to describe. I envy the artist.

Then there is the dreary morning fog and the throaty blast from the funnel and a slippery, greasy sea, with grotesque shapes of other convoy members as they reappear, sometimes just a bridge and mast or just a funnel and a call to each other in their blindness. When everything is wet and slippery and clammy you feel terrible. I've never felt so miserable as the second morning out when I would have been sick if I had had the where-with-all.

The living room is pretty restricted, but sleep comes easily. The food is very good with lovely new bread every day and plenty of eggs. Everything is ridiculously cheap in the ship's N.A.A.F.I., but my money has been in safe custody with the ship's masters and I don't spend much. We keep on gaining time as we go westward and the intervals between meals is sometimes unbearable, but what we lose now we shall gain coming back. It's hard to believe you all are going to bed when we sit down to tea, or that we listen to the midnight news at suppertime!

Sometimes during the day we manage to get an hour's P.T. in, but I'm afraid it is rather a half-hearted attempt and as soon as the instructor turns his back we forget to swing our arms and legs. It does us good, though there's no doubt but idleness breeds laziness and I shall be mortally glad when we get down to some more training.

I hope you weren't worried about the length of the voyage, but circumstances took us from the direct route and the Atlantic is a big ocean where lots can happen in wartime. What matters is if I do eventually get across and am still feeling fine and full of life.

I'm longing to hear from you and how everything is progressing. Most probably I shall have heard by the time you receive this letter. Even Air Mail takes anything up to a fortnight I believe, so the exchange of correspondence won't be very large. I hope Dad is behaving himself and feeling even more his former self. Maybe Hugh has made up his mind as to his wartime calling and I hope for your sakes he will not be too hasty. That little form I filled out more than two years ago has led me into and through some experiences about which I shall have to write a book some day.

And all the time there is the throb, throb, throb of the engines (120 degrees temperature in the engine room!) and the sound of the waves and the up and down of the ship. The sailors are a very decent lot of fellows and live a rotten sort of life I should think. They average 27 days at sea to two ashore and can you wonder they made the best of those few hours! Living in such a tiny world of their own is no life for me! I don't know. You don't seem to belong anywhere at all when at sea. Just a life set apart from all the rest. I hope I don't forget it all by the time I see you again. Won't there be some talking to be done? And I was never one for telling stories.

There is a decent little cinema aboard and I've been several times to see some good films. Sundays we gather aft, and sing a few songs and have a chapter from the Bible read by the Commander. This is of course preceded by a minute inspection and a long, long wait to prepare us for the service. This morning we saw a multitude of wonderful things. First, an octopus went swimming by and then a turtle, a real big one, right on the surface. We then saw the queerest jellyfish with lots of tentacles hanging down and a famous little white sail protruding above the water carrying it along! The sail was semicircular and about one inch by six inches high with variegated edges. We saw a school of dolphins or something very close, and four different kinds of flying fish. The most interesting one was a long pencilly one with double fins each and to gain speed they shot a long stream of water from their bodies. A wonderful sight, seeing about thirty take off at once with long streams flashing behind! There were one or two little ones like butterflies, with fins large and close together and mottled with brown; and the teeny ones that seemed to hop along the water like frogs. It's a wonderful day today with sky clear and the sea calm and sparkling. There was a revolver contest at which we shot rather badly! A lot of other things will have to wait I'm afraid. Another lovely moon last night and we played deck quoits by its light till rather late. Very good fun!

This morning has been the roughest morning of all with seemingly huge waves with white caps sending the bows sky high, and keel coming clean out of the water and spray flying all over the place. Plenty of fellows were soaked to the skin! I've just drawn my Canadian $39.87 and have started learning the value. This letter is coming back on the same ship and we have to finish writing this afternoon, so I'll start closing, hoping all is well with you and wishing the ship a safe passage! Cherrio.

A Follow-up Letter

At last we arrive at our final destination in this huge country where you can travel for days and still have plenty of room to turn around. It's been more than three weeks since we up-tents from Wilmslow and set out to cover half the globe. I trust you received my letters and cablegrams? And I'm looking forward to the day I receive my first letter from you. From the fellows already here we learn that airmail takes about a fortnight and ordinary mail about three weeks, so I shan't be expecting anything just yet. It'll do no good worrying and in our present position, no news may be considered good news.

The whole journey has been extremely various and educational and the temporary stay in Toronto very enjoyable. The first sight of a city lit from end to end was wonderful and that first evening there was very enjoyable. Claud and I went to church and marveled at the appearance and general aspect. Full of color and comfort, they give a first impression of a theatre and this is furthered by the introduction of programs giving the order of service. The service approximates to the Methodist's doctrine and we knew the hymns and tunes. One soon gets accustomed to the right-hand traffic and the wonder of the lights is also momentary.

Toronto from the roof of a skyscraper is worth seeing and the Lake Ontario runs clear to the horizon broken only by the natural harbor. It is a very open city full of trees and parks and wide streets. The houses all have porches usually reached by a stairway and giving the appearance of being attached to the second floor. Especially in the country, these are equipped with rocking chairs and at noon the whole family seems to congregate in the cool shade to discuss the world as it affects them. Everybody is equally friendly from the street cop to the hotel manager, all go out of their way to help and encourage you. We only had three days there and were in some respects unfortunate since those who had had time to make friends were being invited out to meals without fail and week-ends on the lakes, fishing and swimming and riding and thoroughly being adopted by generous families. However, we barely had time to accustom ourselves to the novelty of a new life, when we continued our travel south.

Before I take you south I must tell you of the journey across Nova Scotia and down the St. Lawrence. That early morning filled with mist when we first saw land amid the lazy noise of the foghorn and to the rhythm of the Atlantic. Past the sloops and pine trees into the harbor! We stayed on board until evening when a Canadian National engine of romantic appearance pulled out with bells clanging and numerous whistles blowing.

No one saw us go but we were in Canada and passing through most beautiful scenery. Blue lakes and straight pines and an evening full of red and yellow. Little wooden houses with lights twinkling and tiny stations with no platforms. Real freight wagons and hobos. Girls with baskets of apples giving all you wanted. Worcesters mostly! Wooded hills and little streams, and everything so wonderfully green and fresh. We saw plenty of lumber in the big river but by morning we were going over park land with land partially cultivated on the strip system, and traveling down the St. Lawrence with mountains blue across the water. We passed Quebec about midday on the opposite bank. From then on the scenery did not change much and night fell on numerous level crossings with no obstruction hence the monotonous blast on the steam whistle. Across half the river to Montreal where we stopped for a while about 7:00 P.M. to change engines. We slept as we passed Thousand Islands and dreamt of Fenimore Cooper's heroes.

The train arrived at Toronto about three in the morning, but we weren't woken until five and then paraded to find our kit and bunks. It was a wonderful camp full of amusements and distractions. The food was lovely and I have no doubt that the claim to be the best camp in the world is warranted. We were issued with our summer-issue tunics, which we now find are never worn, but otherwise we just spent money and enjoyed ourselves.

Then we commenced our second stage of the journey through America—to South Carolina, the land of maize, cotton and tobacco. The torrid zone of frogs and hanging moss, peaches and apples. We boarded at about 7:00 P.M. on July 16, 1941, and passed through the Great Lakes peninsular region where we saw grape vines growing in the open. We passed Niagara in the dusk and entered the USA at Buffalo.

We slept along the banks of the Susquehanna and reached Baltimore and Washington, D.C. at noon where we changed trains from the Pennsylvania line to the Seaboard line. I managed to get a glimpse of the Capitol dome and took three photos, one from the rear of the train. They are marvelous coaches with smoking lounges, sleeping cars and dining cars, all air conditioned and beautifully quiet and smooth running. It was beginning to get awfully hot and damp as we went through Virginia. All sorts of new trees and flowers started appearing. Lilies and trumpet roses and the butterflies I saw on one patch of white clover when we halted for awhile were wonderful. I saw

Clouded Yellows, both light and dark, all tame compared with ours, and Hairstreaks with delicate tails and colors. Little speckly ones and queer insects. I must collect as many leaves and flowers as I can to show you all when I arrive home.

We stopped at Raleigh for a while and entered North Carolina still getting hotter and more sticky. It was dark when we reach Camden, our home for ten weeks we trust! Crowds were at the station and cameras were flashing a welcome. By the way, I got my photo stuck in the *Toronto Telegram* with a lot of experiences, etc. included! Cars took us about three miles past the town, which is small with a majority Negro population, to the flying field and bed with clean white sheets! A meal was waiting with milk (we drink a pint with each meal) and fruit for the taking. Marvelous food, but we are getting accustomed to it all now and control our instincts.

In the morning we could have a look around and found we had a lovely big airy room with lockers, polished floors and writing tables, fly nets over the numerous windows and everything beautifully clean. It's terribly hot, as hot as India we were told, and one has to look after one's self to keep fit. We saw the M.O. and received even more kit . . . all American stuff since we are now under the American Air Corp. Discipline is very strict and hours long. Get up at 5:30, breakfast at 6:00, parade for flying at 6:45, dinner at 11:45 and tea at 5:45 with evening study until 9:00. Lights out at 9:30. Weekends are completely off from 12:30 Saturday, but apart from that we remain confined to camp. It needs a lot of adjustment and we are far from settled yet. It's only the second day after all! American drill is awful, but the training is grand. Thirty weeks in three stages, so I shan't be back until March at the earliest, unless I'm eliminated of course and plenty are. But there is no need to think of that!

We met our instructor, Mr. Boykin, with his slow drawl and dry laugh and like him already. We work in fours and two are already friends of mine. The ships are grand and a lot sturdier than our trainers, but I have not been up yet. I've only learned cockpit drill, etc. We start on Monday and they are so safe that they fly by themselves, even straighten out of a spin! So don't worry!

We have to meet the populace yet and hope to do so this weekend. They are awfully hospitable we learned and all the previous intake of English boys have been completely adopted into the kindest of families. Cars and weekends if you don't get behind during the week, when flying is done on Sundays. Sport requires a great effort except swimming, and tennis is rather an effort!

The frogs here create an awful noise during the night and day breaks about 3:00 A.M. We are seven hours in front of you at home which takes a bit of realizing! The variety of insects is extremely large and grasshoppers appear more like highly coloured butterflies.

This is Sunday evening and we've had a marvelous time driving about the countryside and being taken to people's houses. We've already had invitations for next weekend, so many we don't know where to turn. The different cars we've driven in! And all beautiful cars and owned by everyone it seems. We know a very nice fellow who runs a tobacco plantation not far from the airport and he's taken us around a lot. We visited Columbus, the capitol city on Saturday, and went to the dam this afternoon. He has a lot of arrowheads found on the farm, a few of which he has promised to give me. We went to the Methodist church this morning and enjoyed their service and hearty welcome to dinner given in a delightfully informal manner. Invitations to dinner are all the fashion, and I met some awfully nice people, so interested in us British boys as they call us. Am I going to enjoy myself! And the lazy drawl they all use! To hear is to believe and an explanation cannot exaggerate it. It's lovely to hear! I expect I shall absorb a little if I haven't already!
—Cheerio.—

Bea arrives in Washington.

November 25, 1941: My Letter Sent from 5307 Eighth Street, N.W., Washington, D.C.

Dearest Jack,

It seems like an age since I wrote you, but one event has followed upon the heels of another one in such rapid succession that I have hardly had time to turn around. When I received the telegram last Friday to report to the Department of Justice (F.B.I.) on Monday, I dashed down to Westville that very afternoon to get my things there. All day Saturday I was packing and Sunday at 5:00 A.M. I left home for Washington. I have been very fortunate in finding a nice place to stay, since everything here is so terribly crowded. The population here has increased about 200,000 in the last year, so you can imagine what an upset there is.

For two days I have been sitting in classrooms becoming oriented to the F.B.I. I feel very proud to belong to this organization, though I am just one small cog among several thousand. I don't know if you have heard of it at all, but it is to the United States what Scotland Yard is to England. After my return from Birmingham, it was with great joy that I received the news from my supervisor that I was going to be placed in the cryptography department along with one other girl. Only men had previously been employed in that department.

I am a firm believer in the old adage "Never cry over spilt milk," but I can't help regretting that you did not get to come up that weekend as planned. It was a great let-down for me, though I made the best of it with the thought in mind that you would come another time, but now that I have been called up here, it seems such a pity that you didn't come. The idea has been running through my mind that perhaps you can come to Washington before you go back to England. I don't know that the five days in December would give you enough time to warrant your coming then, but maybe you will come through there on your way north and can stop for a while. The first thing that met my eyes when I came out of Union Station when I arrived Sunday was two R.A.F. uniforms.

It made me feel quite at home, and I would like to have talked with them. The week following our visit to Macon, I went over and over in my mind the possibility that I probably should not have gone. But I could not bring myself to regret it. It was good to see you again. Really, that was the only time you and I were ever together. Always you were with somebody else and I was with Arthur—such a strange coincidence. He wanted me to go with him and another couple to Macon for Thanksgiving; said he was going anyway. Did he? Try as I might, I could never make Arthur understand that I could never really care for him. I always liked him, but my feelings did not go beyond that.

Leaving Camden and Westville caused quite a stir of emotions within me. I loved the people and the community so very much, and I was especially fond of the children I taught. But, luckily, I make adjustments easily. Since 1934 when I left home for school, I have been pulling up stakes and moving so much that I have become accustomed to it. I think that I will like Washington, though some time in my life I want to settle down in the good peaceful country permanently. I am not city bred nor have I ever had much desire to live in a city.

Your letter, which I picked up at the post office when I went back to Westville on Friday, was most enjoyable. I have just been reading it over again. Some parts of it cause me to pause and ponder. I suppose both of us take life too seriously for our own good. But it seems impossible to do otherwise. Fate has evidently thrown a monkey wrench into the whole business of life. This war has made such a mess of things. And once it is over, there will be a terrible depression. All of this has to happen to our generation to blight our futures. But I've no doubt that by the time another generation comes along, they will have to go through with the same thing. So it comes over and over. It really doesn't make much sense, does it? I still can't see why we have to let it make a complete mess of all of our lives. In other words, it seems to me that the best thing to do is to try to go on living normal lives and getting what pleasure out of it that we can. My philosophy is a bit jumbled as you can see.

One of the boys we knew in the group at Camden was eliminated and sent to Canada last week. I think it hit him rather hard to leave his friends there. We had him and two others for dinner the last Sunday I was in Westville. We also discovered that the boy who was killed was one of those who rode with us from Columbia that night.

I came up here on a streamline train; it was lovely. It only took about five hours to come. (All along I was reminded of the night we chased down to see the streamline in Camden.) A friend of mine was at the station to meet me. I am living with a couple from my home county. We do our own cooking, housecleaning, etc. It is a lot of fun. In case you do get up to Washington sometime, we have an extra bed and you could stay with us if you wished rather than try to find a room somewhere. I repeat that things are crowded and expensive. Last night I called up several old schoolmates here. They have formed a college club and have asked me to join them; think I will do it.

Wednesday—would you believe it! I slept almost twelve hours last night. I am just catching up with all of that I lost over the weekend. Now I feel wonderful. My working hours for a while will be from 11:00 P.M. until 7:00 A.M. However, I have Saturday, Sunday, and Monday off each weekend.

How is this flying business? If you should fly a plane up here, I should certainly like to take a ride with you, which shows that I have confidence in you. You wouldn't be able to cut any of those stunts, though, or you might have a dead girl when you came down. And how are John and Ted and Eddie Castle? Please give them my regards; come to think of it, maybe I shall send them a card and give my own regards.

Please write to me soon. Naturally I haven't received any mail yet; nobody has had time to get my address and write me. At Westville I usually received some kind of mail almost every day, primarily papers, magazines and the like, but I enjoyed getting it. I feel lonesome not getting a thing. I have quite a bit of work to do, so I will have to stop this gabbling and do it. (Isn't my typing terrible?)

I do a lot of dreaming, but I too believe in prayers. I'll be thinking of you. . . .

Yours, Bea

P.S. When do you leave Macon? You must send me your address as soon as you are transferred and let me know what type of flying you will do when you leave Macon? Do you know when you will leave America?

I Remember

It was on or about April 1, 1944, in the A.M. when I left Janie Wedlock's. Irene may have driven me to Charlottetown's tiny airport. I don't remember. My mental and physical state was such as to render all but the event of leaving itself unimpressionable. Cold, dreary weather, and the sprinkling of snow seemed to fit into the scheme of things. There were no sad farewells.

The trunks and heavy luggage had been sent on ahead, so I had only a small carrying case and a basket, which held one-month-old Richard. Though Jack was a pilot of two years standing, this was to be my first flight. This, under normal circumstances, might have made me nervous, but I felt nothing but relief as that little eight or

70

ten passenger bird took to the air and uttered under my breath a "Thank God" as I gazed out the window at Northumberland Strait.

It was a short flight to Moncton, New Brunswick, where we were to transfer to a larger plane for the flight to Toronto. Nothing of the sort happened. We were taken to a hotel lobby and told the flight was canceled because of a monstrous storm brewing en route. You see, the planes at that time were not equipped for high altitude flying without the use of oxygen masks. We were to proceed as soon as the storm abated. We waited and waited and waited. I changed the baby and gave him the bottle of milk that I had warmed earlier.

As mentioned in my earlier comments about how friendly Canadians had been to us, the flight was made much more tolerable by a helpful stewardess and by a businessman who gave up his room for me upon our arrival in Toronto.

As my supply of formula or milk and diapers was not inexhaustible, I got up at 5:00 A.M. and took the first available train to Goderich, arriving there sometime around mid A.M. I think, feeling weary, sick, in a near state of collapse. It was snowing. Before the train stopped, I could see Jack standing there at the little station.

The war in Europe was winding down, and Jack was transferred to Greenwood in the Annapolis Valley area of Nova Scotia to be trained on 'Mosquitoes,' the fastest plane then in service. I went back to Jean's to stay, and when his training was completed, he was to be posted back to England to await transfer to the Far East.

It was just before leaving for Canada that Richard became sick with bronchitis. Dr. Donnie Royal was sent for, and he proceeded to give the baby a shot. Richard protested loudly and it took me and Mama to hold him still. Dr. Royal said he had never seen a baby put up such a fight!

The bronchitis, incidentally, followed us all the way to Canada and on board the boat. Before we left Canada, however, D-Day arrived and Jack received his discharge papers.

One incident stands out in my memory of that particular stay with Jean and Ira Boss. While Jean and I were having our morning coffee one day, there was a "flash" news item. A Mosquito, flying out of Greenwood, had flown straight through a farm house, wrecking both the house and the plane. The pilot was killed immediately. . . . We both froze and looked at each other, too shocked to speak. Finally I got some words out of my mouth, "But surely they would notify relatives before making a public statement."

Not good enough for Jean and she went into action. "I'll call Ethel and ask her to drive us out there and call Ira to stay with Richard."

We drove down to Greenwood but of course everything was all right and Jack had had nothing to do with the accident—the plane belonging to a different squadron, and while this was going on, Jack hurriedly made plans for Richard and me to sail for England at a time as close as possible to the day he was due to fly to Europe.

Of course he was elated to secure first-class accommodation for Richard and myself a few days in advance of his flight, and we arrived in Halifax shortly after D-Day to see, at first hand, the trashing given the town by sailors celebrating the end of open warfare. The streets were piled high with broken glass and store-fronts to a degree beyond belief. Luckily the staging area was in better shape, and we found our ship moored at the dock and were told to get on board right away. Believe it or not, I was seasick before we even left the shore!

And never was there a cabin less worthy of being designated 'first class' than that one on the Fyffes banana boat—aptly named the USS *Banano*, destined to be part of the very last convoy to cross the Atlantic. We were thrilled nevertheless to get a berth when so much shipping had been lost during the war.

The trip took fourteen days and the weather was frightful. And on top of the terrible weather, Richard remained sick the whole trip. (I later learned a neighbor of ours in Greenlawn was captain of one of the freighters in that same convoy, and he said it was the worst crossing he had ever made, so I don't think we were exaggerating.) To add to our misery, the ship's doctor remained drunk and any complaint was met with the taunt that, "Nobody asked you to come to our country anyway."

We docked and were settled in for a night's rest, but we were rousted out again at about 10:30 P.M. and generally let known that, there in England, it was still a case of the survival of the fittest.

IV
England 1945–1946

There was great excitement when we first saw land, clapping and cheering, and we were told we could put the babies to bed since we were not disembarking until the next day. But this order was soon rescinded and we were told to be ready to disembark as soon as possible—we were to be taken ashore by tender. By this time the babies needed a diaper change and a feeding. And they set up such a howl that we mothers began to think that the steward, the nurse, and the doctor were right—we had no reason to be going to England at this time anyway.

After coming ashore we were taken to a hostel for the night, where we were given a light meal and cots in what appeared to be a huge loft. On the first floor, there was a huge fireplace which offered a friendly atmosphere for fires are lit, even in May, in this part of England. We were allowed very little sleep, being served porridge at five o'clock in the morning. We were then taken by van to the R.R. station skirting the city of Liverpool, which had suffered heavy damage from bombing during the war. From there Richard and I headed for London where my father-in-law met us on the platform of Victoria Station. He said he would have recognized us anywhere and together we headed south for Pulborough in Sussex County, about five miles from the English Channel, and to the village of

Bury, once the home of John Galsworthy, the author of *The Forsythe Saga.* It is there that Dad was raised and from there that he left England to fight the war.

Things didn't turn out too well for any of us in England, what with the lack of housing and having to stay at home with my in-laws. But there are plenty of memories, some of which may have already appeared along the way. Anyway, we were soon thinking about returning to the dear old U.S. of A. and I had started taking notes by this time.

October 5, 1946: Jack, Richard, & I caught the 9:30 A.M. train from Amberley Station to Bournemouth, via Littlehampton, via Ford, via Barnham, via Chichester. At Southampton we caught just a glimpse of the *Queen Elizabeth,* our interest in this ship arising from the fact that we were due to sail on her to New York on November 6. We arrived at Bournemouth precisely on time, 12:22 A.M. Auntie Grace, who met us, had also arranged for our lunch at the Cavendish Hotel, where we were to spend our week's holiday. In the afternoon we went to see Grandma Lunn with Auntie Grace. We then went to Sandhawks. We were immediately "roped in" for a boat ride around Poole Harbor. Tea afterwards at the seaside café, from where we watched the loading and unloading of the ferry. Poor Richard is most unhappy at the idea of going to sleep in a "new beddie" away from Grandad's house.

October 6th & 7th: Almost the whole of these two days was spent at Durley Chine, five minutes' walk from the Cavendish. The weather hung very favorable, and indeed so warm that we all paddled and Richard was able to wear a sun-suit while playing in the sand. Most of the time I spent sitting in a deck chair, knitting. A great snag, we found, was the late breakfast, it being 10:00 A.M. by the old time, as compared to our accustomed 7:30–8:00. As Richard awakened about 6:00, we had four hours on our hands for walks on empty tummies. Concert at the Pavilion on Sunday evening.

October 8: We visited Uncle Chris and Auntie Ethel; also we had the pleasure of meeting "Auntie Jessie," about whom there is plenty to say, but I do not wish to say it!! Peter was still in the hospital and Patsy was staying late at the art school, so we missed them both. I mustn't forget to mention the two dear old ladies who fought so hard to keep our seats on the bus (and succeeded too!) while we had a quick (?) lunch at Bobby's; a cold plate, which cost us about twelve shillings.

October 9: A visit to Cleavers at Poole, very kind and hospitable people. It is to Mr. Cleaver that Jack is indebted for his cello.

October 10: We went, unannounced to West Moors, arriving at "The Crossways," just about lunchtime. But Uncle Frank and Auntie Wyn met the occasion in great spirit, considering meager rations, and they had us not only for lunch, but for tea also. We found ourselves very much at home with them, and the visit was most enjoyable. Richard was beginning to get a cold.

October 12: Lunch with Auntie Grace at Bright's and the 1:30 P.M. train for home; Richard still seeming a bit "off color."

October 15: Had to put Richard to bed, due to rising temperature. At 4:00 P.M. 102 degrees; at 7:00 P.M. 104 degrees. We called the doctor and were told to give him an aspirin. By 10:00 P.M. his temperature had fallen to 100 degrees.

October 16: Richard seemed quite well all day, temperature only rising to 99.8 degrees in the afternoon.

October 17: Richard seemed so well this A.M. we decided to let him out of bed. Upon taking off his pajamas, to our horror we found him covered with a rash! Of course, we immediately thought "measles"—and how long the quarantine, and would we clear the boat in three weeks' time?

October 18: The doctor confirmed our suspicions of yesterday, German measles. But Richard was as well as you please, temperature normal or subnormal, having begged and cried on and off for two days to get out of bed.

October 28: A considerable time had elapsed during which Richard had become quite well again and there was no indication that Jack or I would get his measles. Richard and I went to Arundel in the afternoon, mostly to get "sweets," but we were also fortunate enough to get some cereal, prunes, and canned milk, a great boon to our depleted stock of food. Things seemed to be much worse at this time than when I first came to England. No oatmeal for about a month; meat of very poor quality and only lasting about four days out of the week—which was also true of the bacon.

October 29: A letter had arrived from Cunard bearing embarkation instructions, there had been a great struggle to get three of the trunks off today. Jack also crated my bike and got it off at the same time.

October 31: Florence was supposed to meet me in Arundel, but she rang up to say she cannot. Richard and Granny were off to tea with Mrs. King in the afternoon; Brian, Hugh, Jack, and I went to "Blue Mist" in the evening to see the television. It was enjoyable until I began to get sleepy (about 10:30 P.M.). Also the television screen was very tiring to the eyes, which did not help matters much.

November 2: Brian entertained us—also Dave Ridpath and Ivan—at the Cannaught Theatre, Worthing, where we saw *The Farmer's Wife,* a very good comedy, and well acted. After a cup of tea and buttered bread (too late for cakes!) at the Odeon restaurant, we went to Abbingworth Hall for dinner. Ping-Pong in the recreation room.

November 3: Morning coffee with Mrs. Keay and afternoon tea with the Ridpaths. Washing in between and other odd jobs in preparation for leaving Tuesday A.M.

November 4: Last-minute shopping expedition to Littlehampton. At last I bought the red hat I first tried on about three months ago—53/ or about $10, a very dear do, but I'd become so fed up looking for a suitable hat.

November 5: The day for departure had come at last. There was no real panic preceding the take-off as was the usual case with our moves. Hugh took us to the station at Pulborough to meet the 10:25 train. We had been so busy all along, there had been no time to stop and think—and indeed we did not wish to, for fear some sadness would come over us, or perhaps, some fear of the future that we had chosen for ourselves. But always in our hearts, we knew that it was the right thing and that we and those left at "Hillside" would soon be happier for the change.

We reached Victoria Station about 12:00 noon and after transferring our two cases, cello, and remaining trunk to Waterloo, we went out in search of some place to eat lunch. All the cafés were of the type one usually finds near London's railway stations, certainly not enticing to those whose tummies have been weakened by emotional strain: close, warm, stuffy and smoky, the food being very unappetizing.

Finding our places on the boat train, we settled down wearily for our last train ride in England. People all about us were saying their good-byes, and most of the faces were tear-stained. One little girl across from us, a Jewess

I believe, cried nearly all the way to Southampton, putting us in no good mood for the good-byes we must say at the quay. Scarcely had we finished with the immigration officials when we saw Brian, Hugh, Mother and Dad. Mother was waving "Big Boowoo," whom we had forgotten, a fact that had caused us some concern, as Richard had no other toy and nothing to sleep with. For a while we stood on the dock and talked mostly about the ship; then, as it was getting dark, we said good-bye and went up the gangplank. At 6:00 P.M. we went to dinner, our first meal, and it seemed to us very sumptuous after England's meager rations. We tried to be cautious and sensible, for fear so much rich food would leave us unwell.

Our room was quite nice and very comfortable, except for the heat and stuffiness, due to the fact that we could not open our port hole—too near the water line. Richard had a comfortable crib; there was a small chest of drawers, sink with hot and cold water, electric fan, small closet and fairly good ventilation. Space, however, was precious.

November 6: The boat sailed promptly at 8:15 A.M. We were at breakfast, having chosen the first sitting for each meal throughout the day, our table being No. 55, accommodating six persons. We three had one side. On the other were a Mr. Price from Salt Lake City, Utah; an old lady, apparently deaf and anxious to monopolize the conversation, going to Detroit, Michigan, to join some of her children; and the last one, a young girl going over, after nineteen months of waiting, to marry a Mr. Birdsall of Decatur, Georgia. The food was still good and plentiful; Jack threw discretion to the winds and ate all the butter he wanted!

November 7: A beautiful warm day. We were told we were traveling south toward the Azores. Everybody seemed to be out on deck basking in the sunshine—even the Duke and Duchess of Windsor, whom we passed on the boat deck. She, the Duchess, looked rather old and had bags under her eyes; he wore dark glasses. . . . Jack and I, in short sleeves, played deck games, while Richard played about by himself or collected our disks for us. Some, a good many it seemed, were getting seasick, but our little family was holding out very well. Mr. Price was the only one who joined us for meals, the two ladies having succumbed to seasickness. We found talking to Mr. Price so easy and pleasant, because he seemed to have built up just such a home as we ourselves yearned for—completely self-sufficient as far as feeding his family of six is concerned. He'd been in England three months and was so full of his home and family that now he was going back. Telegram to Brilla.

November 8–9: Not very nice days, rather blustery and damp. And too, the tourist class was confined to one small open deck, the others having been barred against us. Jack was very cross about this and proceeded to outsmart "them"—whoever they are—by following long corridors and finding the "cabin class" staircase, which led us out to all the other decks. We chanced upon another swimming pool, a lovely one, and would like to have gone in, but we did not have our suits.

November 10: Going very slowly; actually wasting time, because we cannot dock until Monday A.M.

V

America

November 11: We arrived at New York City, very early in the A.M. Sometime before we docked, during the early morning grayness, I got dressed and went out to the deck and stood watching the outline of the Statue of Liberty. Tears welled up in my eyes as I thought, "Home at last!" Little did I know of the hardships and struggles we would go through together to build a real home for ourselves.

In the meantime, Jack and Richard had come up on the main deck and we all three began searching in the large crowd on the quay for my brother, Austin. He was meeting us and taking us to my sister, Brilla's house, where we would spend two weeks while looking for a house to rent that we could afford.

Brilla's house was a way-station for family members and friends to hold over until they found a job. Sometimes they were able to repay her, sometimes not. It didn't matter to her. She had a heart as big as all outdoors.

What we eventually found that we could afford was an old house on Hauppauge Road in Smithtown, Long Island. It was without heat except for an old cast iron stove in the kitchen. We bought a kerosene heater for the living room. There was no bathroom, only an outside john some distance from the house. There was only one cold water tap in the house—that was in the kitchen. There was a double stone sink; one half for dishes and preparing food, the other half for bathing. There were no cabinets—only a large pantry to put everything in. The large dining room was unheated and too cold to use in the wintertime. We used an icebox rather than a refrigerator, which required ice every two or three days.

It was in this house, in February of 1948, that I had another baby, a daughter, Carol.

Jack was busy looking for a job. He soon found out that it was useless to look for a job as a pilot (even though this was one of the reasons he came to this country) because he was not yet a citizen and there were thousands of US boys as qualified as he. So, he took the first available job he could find. This was with a building contractor. Mostly all he did was dig cesspools by hand.

I had the feeling that he was unhappy at this point and regretted having left England. When I made this remark to one of my neighbors, she asked, "Why did he come?" And I answered, "For me." He had decided that I was unhappy in England, but I really wasn't to that degree. If only we had been able to live separately from my husband's family, we would have stayed. However, during those post-war years it was impossible to get permission to build a home. We didn't have the money at the time anyway. There had been so much destruction that I doubt we could have found even an apartment to let. So we found ourselves in the States.

Anyway he soon quit the cesspool digging job and started working for a tree company. We had used some of the money that we had brought from England to buy a car. Jack had his heart set on a red convertible, but I persuaded him to buy a used Oldsmobile for $100. With the rest of the money, we then purchased 1.5 acres of land on Dunlop Road in Huntington. Out of the money we saved, being very frugal, we later bought the adjoining 1.5 acres. This turned out to be a very good investment over the years.

Mommie's Day of Rest

January 16, 2:30 P.M.: In about a month's time, I am going to have a baby. I would like to say to myself, as so many women do, "That explains the mood I'm in." But I know perfectly well that isn't true, because there have been other times, under normal conditions, and when I was apparently in the best of health, that I have felt just the same way, hopping mad over everything that meets my eye and threatening in my mind to start divorce proceedings.

"Then," you will probably say when you have read this, "this woman needs to be psychoanalyzed," or, a bit more to the point, "have her head examined." If that be true, then I'll wager the average housewife needs the same treatment; and it is the very fact that she hasn't been to a psychiatrist that makes it possible for her to get up one morning, gay and happy, laughing her silly head off about something that seemed terribly serious yesterday.

My husband has just driven off in our old "Stanley Steamer," which won't begin to steam properly until all the water runs through the big crack in her radiator. His (my husband's) mission? To see about that "rear end" and to see if anything can be done about it. "Rear end" indeed! To my way of thinking right now, there is only one rear end that needs fixing, and I would love to be the one to do it.

Thus began my thoughts when I crawled upstairs

half an hour ago to put a pouting four-year old into his beddie, only to discover that he had been disgustingly neglected after having been on the "pottie" this morning. Down the stairs—and how I hate climbing those stairs when I feel so weary—for warm water and a wash cloth. But all of a sudden, I was steaming with fury, didn't feel at all tired, and no longer in need of the day's rest in bed that Daddy stayed home from work to give Mommie. If I were not angry, I would go good-naturedly about the house putting everything in order: picking up the toys and blocks in the kitchen and living room, and getting out the vacuum to clean up the shavings and sawdust from the living-room carpet. But the way I feel now, they can lie there until they rot!

You see, Daddy built a model house (one day we are going to have a real big one of our own to live in!) in the living room over the weekend, and I, poor idiot, thinking that the carpentry was finished, gave the room a thorough cleaning yesterday, polished the furniture, and altogether spent three hours on it. I had not minded the mess of it, nor fussed about it, because it was really the only place for him to work in, what with no cellar and no other room warm enough except the kitchen. After all, we have to reserve the latter for cooking, eating, and living in, to say nothing of washing and ironing. Too, I always keep reminding myself, they say mothers mustn't get fussy and grouchy about the house being messed up, else the children and the husband won't be happy and it won't be a real home for them. Wherever the mothers come into the picture, I don't rightly know; evidently their pleasure in the home has nothing to do with happiness in general.

And what about the sawdust in the living room now? Ah . . . last night Daddy came home from work almost kicking his heels for joy; he had bought about thirty-six feet of 2 by 2 boards to make blocks for little Richard. I explained, in my most cheerful manner, that I had spent a very exhaustive day washing a few clothes, scrubbing the kitchen floor, changing the bed linens, doing up the dining room a bit, *and* cleaning the living room, and if Daddy would only be so good as to bring the vacuum from upstairs and pick up the bits when he'd finished . . . and what did Daddy's face do? Register a complete blank. To explain: he didn't hear a word I'd said, as is so often the case with Daddy, because of his marvelous powers of concentration!

A couple of weeks ago when I had been trying all evening to get him into some discussion about the coming event, only to have him say several times, "I'm sorry, dear. What did you say?" I at last asked in desperation, "Darling, what on earth is on your mind? You haven't heard a word I've said."

"It's this, baby. They say the fathers suffer more than the mothers, and I surely believe it. Boy, will I be glad when it's over!"

Last night, though exhausted, I could not sleep, and about 1:00 A.M. awakened Daddy and approached him with the subject of a day's rest in bed. "Of course, sweetheart," he mumbled between snores, "I had thought of that myself. I'll stay home so you can just take it easy, stay in bed all day long, while Richard and I do your work for you." He switched off the alarm. That, however, proved to be wasted effort, for instead of the alarm at 6:00 A.M. I heard a little voice call out in great urgency, "Pottie, Mommie!" So, as usual, I bounced out of bed at six.

Determined to have my much deserved day in bed, and assuring Richard that it was the middle of the night and that he must go back to sleep, I crept off into the spare bedroom and closed the door. Half an hour passed, then the little voice again.

"Daddy."

"Yes, Pipsqueak."

"Could I come in your beddie and sing 'I Don't Want Her, You Can Have Her' with you?"

"Not yet."

A few minutes passed and the request was repeated; rejected again, soon repeated again and finally granted about seven o'clock. So began the chorus, ". . . she's too fat, much too fat . . . ," followed by . . . "why'd they have to shoot poor grandma?" Christmas carols and other numbers of their repertoire, the concert ending about eight o'clock, while I . . . well, I was caving in with hunger, but I took courage when I heard the boys going downstairs. There followed the noises attending the jacking up, cranking, and refueling of our 1890 model Boynton kitchen range, which incidentally, is the greater part of our heating system, the smaller part being a two-burner oil heater, which resides in the living-room.

About 8:30 Richard brought up the first course, a toll house cookie. Oatmeal, toast, and coffee followed at nine. When I heard Daddy say, at twelve, that at last the dishes were finished, I thought to myself that it was rather silly of me to lie in bed when there was so much to be done. So, with the idea that I would just lend a hand for a little while, I put on my robe and went downstairs. There was Daddy peeling the potatoes, and where? In the wash basin, of course. Fearing that he might cook them in the same vessel, I ventured to suggest that he mend the mop while I did the potatoes.

In no time flat, the mop was mended, and the next thing I knew the "boys" had emptied all of their six dozen marbles, four dozen new blocks, plus all the old ones, onto the living-room carpet and in the midst of it all had the new choo-choo and the climbing tractor going full speed. In the kitchen I was cleaning up toast crumbs and getting the dinner, which had so obviously been turned over to me. But, though feeling weak and tired (so I thought), I took comfort in the fact that as soon as I'd eaten my dinner, I would be shooed back to bed and persuaded not to get up again until tomorrow morning.

But the best laid plans of mice and men, not to mention women, often go . . . (whatever does happen to them?). Daddy had some few odd jobs to do while Mommie did the dishes, and after that—that is where the news of the "rear end" came into the picture, and a few minutes later, Daddy went off in a cloud of smoke, leaving Richard crying because he couldn't go, and Mommie holding the bag, but still planning to go back to bed!

Having written it down, my anger has reversed itself, and I'm getting that old familiar feeling that life with Daddy and Richard will never grow dull. Perhaps I *can* sleep now. But first I shall put a "don't be nosy" note on my typewriter and leave it on the kitchen table in plain sight.

8:30 P.M. Daddy sees my note and, as I'd hoped, read what I'd written. His reply—"Phooey!—the way you women are always threatening us poor men with divorce!"

The result—I had to do the dishes and clean the living room as always. Then came shaving time.

"Darling, where is my razor?"

"I'm sure I don't know. I haven't seen it since I cleaned there two days ago."

"Oh, I remember, Richard had it this morning shaving the walls. Richard, where is my razor?"

"Oh, it's there, Daddy," came a sleepy voice from up-stairs, "I hid it."

"Yes, but where?"

"Under the cushion in that brown chair in the living room!" Chuckles from both parties.

And what do you suppose Daddy is doing now? Sand-papering the new blocks . . . yes, you guessed it, *ON THE LIVING-ROOM CARPET!* Now I ask you, "What are men and boys made of, made of!"

1948

May: Having obtained a deed for 1 1/2 acres of land on Dunlop Road, between Greenlawn and Huntington, Long Island, New York, we begin our sure-to-be-long struggle for our own home—the little place where we can unpack our trunks for good and—if space becomes too precious—throw them away! This is the thing we have worked toward throughout the six years we have been married, but I must confess we are not thrilled, having been more or less forced to take something short of what we wanted. Further waiting seems futile, and to us at the moment, the thing of greatest importance is to build a home for our family.

June: The work has begun. The first of the month, Jack did the necessary digging to have the water main tapped and a meter installed. All of which involved money—more than we had anticipated.

On Friday, June 11, the cellar and cesspool were dug, the latter causing us some concern: eighteen feet and still no sign of sand, only "hard-pan." There is about one foot of topsoil, very nice loam, two feet of brown clay and then the hard-pan. On the evening of the 11th, after much deliberation (I with my visions of cesspool trouble through-out the years and the fear of having to be forever "stingy" with water; Jack with his concern about the difficulty of building such a deep cesspool), Jack called Mr. LaMay and instructed him to dig no further.

Saturday, the 12th, Jack arrived on the scene to find a hole, twenty-seven-feet-deep, with sand at the bottom! Gravel had been discovered while rounding out the bottom. Mr. LaMay settled for $120, $62 for the cellar, $58 for the cesspool.

June 13: Rain practically all day. Partial clearing in late afternoon. So we decided to visit our "holes." The deluge had washed a pile of dirt into the cesspool. All about was like a quagmire. Our Italian neighbors from the city were out for the weekend in their one-room shack—two sisters, their father and husbands and eight children. They went out of their way to be friendly, gave us some kind of "greens" and strawberries; complained about other adjoining neighbors putting up fences! And all the time, I'm thinking how much I want to get a fence or hedge around our place before they build next to us, and—

June 15 is a good day. Jack and Bill began laying the blocks in the cesspool.

June 20: (Sitting in the sunshine—back lawn): The past week has been rather a discouraging one, notwithstanding the fact that the cesspool is nearing the top. There has been so much rain and in the middle of the week the car went on the blink. It was supposed to be done on Friday night, then Saturday night, then Sunday A.M.—and the last report said, "Call for it Sunday noon." Jack went off on the bike this A.M., hoping to take it on the train to Greenlawn, do a day's work, and cycle the four miles to the garage for the car. I only hope it's ready!

On Friday, Terry and Elaine came over to swing in Richard's swing. They were begging to ride his bike. "Okay," he says. "Terry, take four turns around the path; Laney, take four turns; I take four turns, then you can go home!"

Today is lovely—blue sky and breezy, but rather chilly for this time of the year. The garden seems to be coming on fairly well. Richard is collecting fallen apples in his trailer; Carol is asleep. Tomorrow she will be four months old.

Evening: Austin and May brought Jack home about 7:00, the bike tied on the back. No car, of course, but ready for sure on Tuesday!! Jack finished the cesspool, thank Heaven, and dug a bit of the trench for the drain pipe.

June 21: Continued good weather, of which I took advantage to do the week's wash; also some gardening—found one small green tomato. Everything needs some attention. Jack returns a little before 9:00 P.M. very much out of sorts. It had taken about three hours to dig three feet for the footing; he'd walked to the station, walked—almost run—to Morganberger's for his lunch box, barely made the train, forgot the loaf of bread in Smithtown and had to return for it on the bike. Home at last, his lunch box flew open and spilled all the gooseberries he'd picked for a pie. Poor Daddy is very discouraged.

June 22: *Rain.* Jack went to work, but spent most of the day digging the trench for the footing; almost completed it—in much better spirits.

June 23: *Rain*—buckets of it! No work for Jack. We went to the bank to negotiate for a loan, but we found they would let us have nothing on the strength of our assets in the Bank of England—a great blow for Jack, who is really in the dumps now. The car was finally finished this afternoon. Jack finished the trench for the footing. He has described it as a disastrous day for us! Trombley came over in the afternoon.

June 26: Perry, Annie, Ted, and Jones arrive for a week's visit. Nice weather.

June 27: Dinner with Brilla. May has an infected foot.

June 28: The footing for our cellar has been finished. Also, most of the digging completed. Very hot day. Family has dinner with me.

June 29: Another uncomfortably hot day. Poor Carol cried nearly all day with the heat. Dinner at May's. Visit Odell and Lucy Thompson in afternoon.

June 30: Still warm, a little less humid. Jack finishes the trench (six feet deep I believe) from the house to the cesspool. Comes home soaked from perspiration and red with the clay.

July 1: Brilla, Annie, Cat, Richard, Bobby, and I visit our "house." Jack is there working; finishes the trench from the water main to the cesspool. Nice day, a little rain about 6:30 P.M.

July 2, 3: Lovely days, breezy and low humidity. Walked to town for a bit of shopping on Saturday P.M.

July 4: Austin gives Jack a day and they begin laying the blocks for the cellar. Another beautiful day . . . all went well, except one corner had to be torn down and realigned.

July 5: Austin gives another day and all corners were laid and found to be level and perfectly square. I believe Jack is beginning to feel that the building of a house *is* within the range of possibilities . . . very hot and humid, so much so that Austin had to quit work at one point and lie down in the shade. Also, Jack realized at this point that one should wear gloves while handling cement blocks. His fingers had begun to bleed.

July 6: Hot and humid. Shopping with Brilla in the A.M. Also lunch with her. Thunder showers begin about 4:30 P.M.

July 11: Richard goes with Jack. May and Bobby spend the day with me. May gives me a Toni.

July 18: Jack comes home early to take me over to see the house—or rather, the cellar. It is completed up to the seventh row of blocks, including the garage.

July 24: Blocks finished, also some filling-in done.

July 25: Canned beans. Richard comes home not feeling very well and soon is doubled up with a tummy ache. Eats no supper.

July 26: Richard and Carol to Dr. Molinoff. Both perfectly well. Carol gets her first needle for diphtheria and tetanus; weighs 16 lbs, 15 oz!

July 30: Bought lumber for first floor.

August 1: This is the month Jack has taken off to "get the roof on," more or less. And, naturally it begins to rain today. Jack mends my bike on the back porch. In the afternoon we went for a drive and attempted to "get lost" in San Remo. What a dump!

August 2: Carol to the doctor again. Whooping cough needle. Cloudy but not rainy.

August 3: Thunder showers all day. Very little done on house. Windows and two doors ordered—over $500.

August 4: Sub-floor almost finished.

1950

May: She was only two and had a very limited vocabulary. In fact she spoke in a sort of shorthand made up entirely of brief forms. Only a mother's patience could have brought about an understanding of such utterances as "My-T," which meant she had a tummy ache, and "doal, orter," which meant she wanted the stool by the sink so she could get her own drink of water. Each morning after our old car sputtered away out of sight, she would point out the window and say "Dadee, car, erk," to which I must respond, "Yes, Daddy's gone in the car to work." And when the school bus arrived to take Richard to kindergarten, it was "Jar ghoul buh," and Mommie must say, "Yes, Richard's gone to school in the bus." Then she would play with her dollies and blocks, and have tea parties at her little table and sometimes go for "alks" with Mommie.

On Sunday mornings when Dadee was home she would say, as soon as she finished breakfast, "Jar, Dadee, me, alk. Mommie, no." I knew she'd rather go with Dadee for a walk because he never said, "Mind you don't fall!" nor "Oh, dirty, throw it away!" Dadee let her run as fast as she could down the hill, and he let her pick up old tin cans, and when she got tired, Dadee would throw her over his shoulders and bring her home piggy back.

Most days Dadee was gone, but after she had her nap and Jar came home from school and they played rough games for a while, she began to go in ever so often to Mommie and say, "Dadee, dome, erk," and Mommie would say "Not yet." In a little while, Mommie would look at the clock and say, "Dadee should be coming home any minute now," and she and Jar would run to the window and watch, and sure enough, in almost no time at all, there was Dadee's car coming into the driveway. She and Jar began to skip and clap their hands. As soon as Dadee came in, they would say, "Bang, bang!" which meant Dadee had been shot and must fall down dead. Then they would jump upon his back and go for a horsy ride all over the house. Dadee was the most wonderful father!

June: Carol: "Mommie, me go Balaa houch." (Mommie, I want to go to Barbara's house.)

Mommie: "You can't go to Barbara's house with measles!"

Carol: (folding her pajamas around her tummy, where the measles were most pronounced.) "Balaa no me chee meage!" (Barbara won't see my measles!)

Richard returned from town with a new cowboy hat and whistle (green and yellow).

Carol, standing up in bed, very excited, says, "Me on try cobee hat!"

English relatives visiting us were delighted with our radio advertising. One morning I came down to find my father-in-law almost in stitches. He had just been relating the story of the housewife who had had a thief break into the house and steal her most prized possession—a package of some brand of soap flakes. In his efforts to get away quickly, the thief had fallen from a window to the ground below with a "thickening sud."

1952

November 2: There was beautiful music—a philharmonic playing Mozart. I was in the kitchen doing these last minute things that always seem to crop up every night before going to bed.

"Come on, Mommy," said Daddy, "Let's turn out the lights and listen for a few minutes."

"Well, okay." I hesitatingly left the last job unfinished. We settled down on the couch. Daddy brushed my hair, as he often did evenings while we listened to music.

Through the three small panes of glass in our front door, I could see the street light—but very faintly through the thick fog. The fog! Suddenly, I was remembering those fogs of Yorkshire, where, in November, one always seems to be looking at the sun through a smoked glass.

The mood of music changed. I was still watching the street light outside, and suddenly I was standing under a streetlight in Wick, a suburb of Littlehampton, on the channel. I had come on the bus to have tea with Florence—poor distraught Florence. My heart was heavy with sadness for her and little Bruce. The fog was so thick that it seemed to bear down on my shoulders. Never before had I felt so alone or such a foreigner in England.

People have asked me if I liked England. I, who am steeped in English literature and history? Who even took a class in Chaucer? Who could **not** like England, with her hedged-in lanes and the 'lay-bys' (pullover spaces along the narrow country roads)? With her charming old villages? Yes, I was born to live in England.

My husband said, "To be truly English, you must learn to ride a bike." So he took me up the road to Grey & Rousel (I wondered why we were walking). They sold cars and bikes. Jack picked out a couple of bikes and told me to try them out. "But why?" I asked. "Because you are going to ride it home." "But I've never ridden a bike," I pleaded. "Then it's time you did!" That was that.

I rolled it over to the right side of the road and put my feet on the pedals. Home was downhill so it went fast and straight . . . into the briar patch. Unlike Brer Rabbit, that really wasn't where I wanted to go. "You're doing great! Now get on again." I got on again, made more progress, but still landed in the briar patch. A third time Jack said, "Get on one more time." By now I was beginning to get the feel of it and told myself, "I'll ride this thing if it kills me."

And away I went and made it all the way home, feeling a great sense of accomplishment. After that Jack and I had many pleasant rides together in the English countryside. We went on picnics and rambled off the lanes into the famous English parks, one of which was surrounding Arundel Castle.

When we moved to America, Jack crated up my bike and we brought it with us, but I was unable to continue riding because of Jack's work schedule and the birth of my second child. That was the end of my bike riding.

Later, when we moved to Dunlop Road, Jack began to teach me how to drive our pickup truck, but he was a lousy teacher and I asked one of the ladies at church to teach me instead. I had to learn to drive because I needed to take courses at the State University in Farmingdale, New York to get my teacher's license renewed. I had to do this in order to begin teaching in the fall of 1954. My working plus an increase in Jack's salary made it possible for us to buy our first new car, a 1954 green Chevy, which cost only $1400.

1953

September 5: Carol came in from her play. "Mommy, I've got a daisy flower for you." I was curious to know what her idea of a daisy flower was: a small bunch of wilted clover. I was going to put them in the egg cup by the sink, but found in that two small smooth white rocks. "What's this?" I asked. "Birds eggs of course!" Indignant that I shouldn't know.

Richard still running a slight temperature and also suffering from infections on his feet—poison ivy or athlete's foot? Goodness knows!! Daddy awfully tired and a little grumpy. Mommy—just tired!

September 9: School opens. Carol's first day. First egg from Richard's chickens. Very thrilling for all. Great activity getting new straw for nests. Carol says, "Every time we hear a chicken cackling, we'll know we have another egg, huh, Mommy?"

September 11: Richard is very keen to get interesting hobbies and make collections. Some incentive from school. This P.M. he made a butterfly net, rather crude, but workable and most satisfying to him, as he promptly caught a moth!!

1954

January: We were watching *Victory at Sea* on television. Carol, much engrossed, upon seeing a sailor climbing the rigging said, "Holy Smokes, Daddy! There's a man climbing up to the scarecrow's nest!"

June: Mrs. White showed me some very colorful abstract art work of Carol's. "You should keep this, Mrs. Bollam. It's beautiful and she'll never do it again. Modern artists try to copy these things but never succeed. Next year she'll start making things that look like '*things*.' Yes. I'll frame it for you; I have just the right frame for it. . . ." So you see I did—sort of—keep a diary!

Date Unknown

"*Now* what's the matter?" he asked me. "I'm having some horrible thoughts and I'm enjoying it, so please don't talk to me."

1955

October: Sitting in the Commack faculty room talking: the kindergarten teacher is telling about one of the morning children who is talking about changing to afternoons. She told Mr. Morey, "I hope not, as I have already entered him in my register." "You have!" he seems astonished. "After all, from kindergarten—where could they go?" Mr. Clark seems to consider the question. "Um—high school, maybe?"

A lot of us teachers are afflicted with the disease of "forgetting to pass out notices." I believe that is particularly true of those of us who have afternoon sessions.

On the afternoon of October 18, I stayed a few minutes after school to clean up, discovered in my desk the sealed envelope that I was to have given Raymond for his mother. It concerned a polio shot, I knew, and it might be important that she get it today. I would just have to take it by.

After waiting several minutes for a break in the traffic, I crossed to the other side of the turnpike and headed west. Upon approaching the first light, instead of going straight as usual, I put on my blinker indicating a left turn and came to a full stop. A car facing me was also stopped, waiting to make a turn to my right, the lane to the far left facing me seemed clear for a considerable distance. I cut my wheels to make the left turn. In that horrible instant, I realized that a car was bearing down upon me at considerable speed. In what seemed only a part of a second, I felt the impact of his car against mine. I somehow managed to steer the car toward the parking lot, but I couldn't clear the rear end of the station wagon.

I wasn't hurt, but I had a sort of sick feeling inside. Several people had arrived by the time I got out, including the man in the car that had hit me. "Thank God, he isn't hurt either," I thought. "Better call the police," someone said. One man with a very kind face was saying, "I've been all through it, except you're luckier than me. I turned over."

Everyone asked, "Have you got insurance?" and when I'd nod my head, they would go on, "Oh, you're all right—nothing to worry about." That's what the trooper said too, when he arrived five minutes after the accident. "You're both insured—nothing to worry about." Someone said, "You certainly are calm." I was surprised myself that I wasn't more shaken. As if by magic a man arrived with a tow truck.

1956

March 19: The worst snowstorm in eight years has descended upon us and might prove far worse than the one in '48. Elsa and I barely made it home from school last Friday, but by Saturday P.M. we were able to go to Huntington and do some shopping. However, never dreaming it would begin snowing again on Sunday, we only got a few things to "tide us over" the weekend.

We "rationed" our milk and bread at breakfast and lunch. This P.M. the snow plow finally got through, moving laboriously and blowing the snow as it went; also, Mr. Schobel's boy arrived with some milk. Fortunately, the electricity is still on, but up to fifty-five-mile-an-hour winds are predicted for tonight and at 3:30 P.M. it is still snowing.

Richard, Carol, and Daddy have been out on two excursions; during the last one, they measured drifts up to five feet.

Announcements have already been made to the effect that schools will be closed tomorrow.

1959

It is a drizzly March Monday morning, fine rain with a few snowflakes interspersed, the death and life struggle between winter and spring. (Two days ago we awakened to find it had snowed considerably during the night.) We eat our breakfast of porridge and bacon leisurely, the children being home for Easter holidays. They make their usual uncomplimentary remarks to each other (is that *really* natural for brothers and sisters?). Dad says somebody's got to find some *work* for Richard to do.

Dad takes his book and retires to the bathroom. He is allowed a few minutes before the protests begin. "Hey, Dad, are you going to spend the day in there?" Bang, bang, bang! "Hurry up, Dad!!" "I'm next." "You are *not*. Didn't you hear me say I was next after Dad!" Bang, bang, bang!

Chummy is scratching on the cellar door. He now sleeps in a box in the corner of the garage. Somehow he seems to know it is a special privilege. He seemed to find sharing his house with Laddie unbearable and would, I believe, have died had he not been relieved of it.

April 2: It has rained in torrents today. I finished *The Yearling*. Many of its descriptions and conversational expressions were very reminiscent of the South of my childhood, which I gather was not *too* far removed from the time of Jody Baxter. Brilla called to say she was going to the hospital at 3:00 P.M. and would be operated on by Dr. M. tomorrow A.M. "Have you talked to Austin?" I asked,

100

whose opinion of Dr. M. is that he "wouldn't let him operate on his dog."

I was to be at Mrs. Hall's at 1:00 P.M. for the Women's Organization Meeting. I could not seem to find the house, got out to ask at a couple of places, became thoroughly wet, hair hanging in strings; came home to pot tomato seedlings, a very pleasant way to spend a rainy afternoon.

It has been the kind of day that always brings up the question "Dad, can we go to the movies?" It only needs a "maybe" and a little prodding to make it a reality. As I find most movies intolerable and went to my "annual" one about three weeks ago, I wasn't even asked. I like a quiet time to myself occasionally; I am very apt to spend it reading, cleaning out a drawer, a closet, or just anything that strikes my fancy.

The "peepers" are out; the grass has become green almost overnight, though I have only seen two robins.

April 29: The last two rainy days I spent in bed with a heavy cold, getting up only to do the necessary cooking, housecleaning, etc. Today the sun is shining in a cloudless sky. I am staying in bed only for a couple of hours.

Part of my time has been spent reading *The Gold of Troy,* the life story of the archaeologist, H. Schliemann, who pushed himself relentlessly, but with no true direction. This led me, of course, into my chief "thought" subject: what is truly worth doing and worth having in this life! What are the important things, *really?* Health? Happiness? Money? Love? Austin argues that money could have solved almost any problem that he has had to face in life. The doctor who treats him for his ulcers (which happen to be very bad at this time) tells him ulcers are definitely a psychopathic ailment. "You should try to change—don't let things bother you," he advises.

"Change!" says Austin. "Just like switching off a light—and I've been myself for forty-six years already!"

I contended, and always have, that one *can* change with a little effort. "Sure," replies Austin, "*If* you've got plenty of money. Then if things at home annoy you, you can just pack up and take off for a few weeks." I do not agree. Only the environment is changed—not one's self. Henry agrees.

Jack argues that happiness should not be one's aim (since the hope of attaining it is not in line with reality?). He anticipates, rather, that things are going to turn out badly with the thought that if they actually *do,* one knew it all along and is in no way disappointed; whereas, if it turns out well, what a wonderful surprise!!

I feel that one can change his whole viewpoint toward life through a systematic study and awareness of the world about him—his immediate world, not some far distant lands that he can never hope to see. As I sat up in bed yesterday, watching the low-hanging sweeping branches of the willow, it occurred to me that I might spend the rest of my life studying the great debate that continues even today: which has the greater impact on human development, environment or heredity?

April 19, 1962: Nature Observations

During the latter part of March, we had some beautiful warm weather. I should know better, but I planted about ten rows in my garden. Since then, it's been either cold rain or cold fair.

Last year a pair of finches became very interested in an arbor vitae just outside my kitchen window. It was long past nesting time, so I could only surmise they were staking out a claim for future use. About three weeks ago, they were back, nosing around and carrying on a running conversation about the proper way to begin a house.

"Lucky things!" I remarked. "No zoning board—no building permit."

A couple of days later, they got down to business, or rather *she* got down to business. She did all the work, collecting twigs and building the nest. He followed her wherever she went, but always came back empty-beaked, flew directly to the maple tree nearby, and the minute she began arranging the twigs, he burst into his song.

After about the third day of this happy routine, we noted some cowbirds walking along the path. Now the female cowbird is the kind of mother who, were she human, would leave her baby on somebody's doorstep, or be hauled into court for neglecting her children. She sneaks on another bird's nest, lays her egg and goes on her merry way.

So it was no surprise that after poor Mrs. Finch had finished her nest—it took about a week—and she had the misfortune of having most of the nest-lining feathers stolen from her by English sparrows and we found two cowbirds eggs in her nest.

The pair of mallard ducks is back this year, arrived two or three weeks ago, he handsome and brilliantly feathered, she quite dull. They are so tame that when we sit on the lawn, they come up to us for food and water and sit down for a visit.

The starlings are as brassy and cocky as ever, acting as if the world is their oyster. Jack says they are the Yankees of the bird world.

He came in one day with his hands cupped together and said, "Guess what I've got!" We took a peek and saw the tiniest female kinglet. She was sitting by the barn door and didn't utter a protest when picked up.

One day he wrote a piece about our favorite creatures and it seems appropriate to include it at this time. He called it. . . .

Swallows

They weigh less than an ounce it would seem, yet within that tiny scull they possess the wherewithal to navigate a course through the twigs and branches of any particular tree at speeds that might translate into many hundreds of miles-an-hour in the human frame of things and ruffle not a single feather nor dislodge a single leaf in the doing of it. They fly over thousands of miles of hostile territory and unerringly pinpoint a certain square inch of the globe as their nesting place. They remain loyal to their family for the most part (there is always the maverick in nature). The dominant male becomes their leader and scout—flying on a week ahead to confirm the availability of last year's building site. They move in pairs—always in pairs—and remain loyal to their mate as well as the group. They are swallows—the undisputed aristocrats of the bird kingdom.

We first became acquainted with this autocratic bunch, or rather they with us since they accepted us—only barely mind you—some few years ago. Since then their arrival has become the most important event of the season and looked upon as a harbinger of good or bad events since their natural sagacity has repercussions beyond human cognition—no need for insurance on a building selected as a building site—it's safe from fire or flood—I'm not sure about the Building Department, but I wouldn't be surprised!

Our first settler happened to be the feistiest of all our

104

acquaintances, and many a battle with our son, although lost, made him even more feisty than before. I never once saw him lose his dignity when he wound up covered with mud in the corner of the greenhouse. As soon as he was dried off, he was up again and back in the fray with added fury. Their method of attack was out of the sun in a high-speed dive copied by the Germans during the war followed by the nearest of misses it's possible to imagine and a click resembling the cocking of a rifle as one's hair was ruffled by the after shock. Pity the poor crow or sparrow should they enter their air-space without permission—the whole group was put into action in seething mass of violated pride.

Nest building was a consummate craft and called for after hour classes, but the finished product was durable and architecturally sound. At one time I hung a ladder on two metal spikes driven into the garage wall—just a plain old spike with no head and nothing to make a hold on, and this pair decided to be a little different and move out of the barn. It was against the rules since these doors had to be closed from time to time. So the battle began—they building at the night—me knocking down in the morning. This went on for a couple of weeks with no surrender when I had the idea of hanging an empty can on the end of the spike so that it would rotate if any building went on. So ingenious was this move on my part that I no longer even bothered to look in their direction for several days. When I did I was confronted by a fait accompli—a finished nest and two newly laid eggs! Notch another one up for the birds! We did win a few victories, but they were mostly pyrrhic victories and with a level playing field, there was never any doubt as to the eventual outcome. You see I always assumed they were the more valuable contributor to the scheme of things since they knew exactly what they were doing and we did not.

Early on when they overbuilt and the place resembled a chicken house, I closed the barn doors on them—for

105

Swallow patrol

good, I told myself. But the old patriarch knew me better than that and he and his mate just sat on the utility line—staring—staring—staring, day after day as though I was some sort of abominable pariah. After being stared at for a couple of months, I was ready to come to terms and never closed the doors on them again. They are examples of all I would like to see in the world. They always build in the same place and seem to prefer that I knock down their old nest so they could build a new one each year (I may be wrong about this, but I somehow believe it to be the case.) They remain an inseparable pair—it never even enters their heads that it should be any other way. He was the undisputed head of the group and as such possessed the most strident warnings of possible danger (mainly the proximity of our teen-aged son). There finally came a day when he could no longer play his part and we found him dead on the floor beneath his nest. His mate sat there for three days before she also fell. I still find it hard to believe!

Perhaps the most remarkable feature of swallowdom, though, is the manner in which they feed their young. A brood consists of five chicks, usually, and in order to distribute the food evenly, they rotate by instinct so that each youngster gets a turn at front and center. At the approach of maturity, nevertheless, we almost always have a youngster who wants to fly before he is able to do so and we have one on the floor and there is nothing we can do about it since it soon exhausts itself in futile attempts to take off. Then we have the one who never wants to fly until it's forced to do so on account of no food. My! Oh, my!

When I cut grass sometimes and stir up all kinds of insects and the living is easy, my swallows fly with me and show off their stuff. They do lazy eights and immerman rolls and cut the mustard in the most intriguing ways. Flying low, they make a point of missing my machine by a quarter of a wing length—if that. Brassy,

Cocky, Friendly; they go out of their way to make me feel at home—part of the family, so to speak.—In the know.

1961

April 24: Lillian came up from North Carolina to see Annette off for Germany. They were dumbfounded at the vastness and complexity of Idlewild Airport. I went to Smithtown for lunch and conversation. The latter quite naturally centered around the folks "back home," living and dead, family jokes told and re-told.

The McLambs were our neighbors back in the early years of my life. They were full of fun and laughter, always laughing at themselves, relating every stupid thing one of them did. One, Oscar, was a kleptomaniac and until this day, it's a common joke among the other members of the family that everything one wants is hid when he comes. Once Oscar spent the night with brother Elmon, whose wife was astonished to see him pull off his trousers and put them under his pillow. "You must have a lot of money in your pocket," she remarked. "Not a cent," he answered, "but I want my trousers to put on in the morning."

Another time Oscar invited his Uncle Lloyd to a chicken fry down by the river. "Come on down early," he said. A few minutes after he got there, Oscar disappeared, but he was talking with some folks and gave it no attention. Soon Oscar was back with five nice chickens, which were plucked and fried accordingly. . . . When Uncle Lloyd counted his chickens the next morning, he was five short. My mother said, "I'm afraid to sun my chamber pot when Oscar's in the neighborhood!"

We talked too of Aunt Amelia and her family. I remembered the girls, but I could not recall the visits of the boys, who sawed the tails off our pigs, sawed the spokes out of the cart wheels, shooed the setting hens off their nests, and mixed up the eggs—some that should hatch in two days, some in two weeks, etc.

I Remember

When I was a little girl I used to walk alone in the woods a lot, during the winter months when farm chores were fewer. Mostly they were light-hearted times, and I derived from the walks a kind of quiet joy. But on occasion I would be overcome by an unaccountable feeling of sadness and sorrow, which to me seemed to envelop the whole world. I would write sad little commentaries and poems, which I hid in a hollow log. And at times when my heart was especially heavy, I would go in a little clump of bushes, kneel down and pray. Everything seemed to be just between me and God. And though my religion was a serious matter to me, it was very private. I never spoke of it to others, mainly, I suppose, for fear they would laugh at me.

I was gentle, tender-hearted, non-aggressive, and, I must confess, would not fight back with any spirit whatsoever upon those rare occasions when I was spoken to harshly. Mostly my disposition toward peace was known and respected.

This afternoon I went for a walk, again feeling like a heavy-hearted little girl seeking communication with God, up and down the hills of the dairy farm, thoughts tumbling over themselves in my mind. Had our marriage been one sorrowful mistake? He had reminded me at breakfast of a comment he had made a few days earlier to the effect that perhaps we *were* on the right track, though he had so often wondered if he had not made the wrong turn back there. By that, he said, he meant our marriage, and that I must have wondered many times too. It is true, I have.

You see, we both had a disadvantage in our youth: a considerable lacking of worldly experience and an unrealistic attitude toward marriage. We were from different countries, different family backgrounds, and knew—oh, *so* little about each other—having been together only about a half dozen times! With so many strikes against such a marriage, surely it must have been under the watchful eye of God to have been sustained these twenty years, though God and religion seem to have been given a small corner indeed in this household.

1965

January 11: Carol and Jack return from England. I had made three calls to the airport. First I was told Flight 103 was canceled, passengers reaccommodated on Flight 72. Second, they were not on that passenger list. Third, they were not on the next list. In desperation, I had Flight 72 rechecked and found them. I called Herman. We only had forty-five minutes to get dressed and get to the airport. They arrived about 7:30 P.M.

January 26: Everywhere the snow is piled up in soggy heaps—higher than one's head in places. Carol had a day off from school (between terms). Linda and Anne came for lunch and later wanted to go to the shopping center. I did not feel very well, but I went with them anyway. Bought a blanket (much needed) at Macy's. Rich has his last exam tonight. He plans to go to Connecticut to-

110

morrow and come home Friday or Saturday. Jack worked all day in the greenhouse. He expects the first cuttings tomorrow. Jerry came by at tea time—filled us in on his bursitis and his concern at being "almost forty."

January 30: Tomorrow I begin teaching again. I am very apprehensive about it and dread the thoughts of having to go through the business of trying to do two jobs well and not being able to do it. I did so want to get the household organized this winter and help Carol arrive at a more orderly existence. I feel—I know—it is so important and I get so terribly frustrated that I sometimes come close to the breaking point. And there is no understanding or support from Jack.

1966

April 9: You wonder why I write things down? I don't know—perhaps to ease my heart. Today I have been forcefully struck with the idea that I want desperately to die—now, this minute—not to be dramatic or to bathe myself in self pity—but with a view that suddenly life is futile and purposeless. I have come to the end. I could not take my own life, but to lie down and have done with it, peacefully and without fanfare—Gad, that is a thought to dwell upon! Whether or not there is a hereafter doesn't really concern me at this point. Perhaps if there is a soul, it dies bit by bit as does the body, until both dissolve in dust.

Remembrances: an Update

The previously described period in my life, which covered several years, was fraught with events that tended to make me depressed: I had miscarried a baby, I had the feeling that Jack was unhappy in America and that he no longer loved me (regretfully, I even went so far as to burn a trunk full of love letters he had written to me over the years), and our house and business was being built piece by piece as we could afford it (I felt it would never end!). I was under such pressure while I was trying to teach full time, help Jack with the business and take care of the children, that I remember an often repeated dream I had: I was unable to find the time to get dressed and would go off in the morning to teach with no clothes on, often wearing roller skates. At least it was comic relief during a difficult time. As I look back upon this period of my life, I begin to realize that those were my menopausal years. There has been a complete turnaround in my feelings and in my relationship with Jack. I now have no doubts that we love one another. Since I became ill, he has been loving and devoted, the very best caregiver I could hope for. (I've thrown away that little "black book"!)

1961

July 30: Perhaps the most lasting story I heard today is about my sister Lillian. She was asked if, of all her thirteen children, there was one she loved better than the others. "Yes," was her unhesitating reply. "Well, which one is it?" "Oh, it isn't always the same one," she said. "What do you mean?" "It's the one who is sick or in trouble. That is not always the same one."

1969

January 6: We were on our way to the airport before daylight this A.M. We had about a two-hour wait before our plane took off for St. Thomas. I felt weary and sleepy and was anxious to get the trip over with so I could relax. The flight was somewhat bumpy due to clouds from a large storm system over the Atlantic.

The temperature at St. Thomas was in the 80s and our woolen jackets had to be shed immediately. We took a taxi to the marina where we crawled aboard a small, beaten-up ferry for the trip to Tortola. What we had been told in New York would be $2.75 became $3.50 each. We were not long in discovering that rates for everything were high and that food prices were much higher than in New York.

We arrived at Long Bay about 4:00 P.M. and found our cottage comfortable and attractive, with the conveniences of refrigerator and stove. Though we could get meals at the restaurant there, they would cost us about $18 per day—which is ridiculous. So we planned to cook for ourselves.

January 7: After swimming before breakfast, we inquired about transportation to Road Town, a few miles away. There were no buses and no bikes available for rent. We were told bikes were useless on the steep, rough roads and paths, and I believed them. It seemed the only way to get about was by taxi or by "minimoke." So we decided to rent a minimoke for a couple of days so as to see the rest of the island and buy some supplies. Mr. Penrose, who was going into town on business, offered to take us and drop us off at the bank where we were to be met by a man with a minimoke. We went for a ride in it and Jack had a go at the wheel, thinking he would go and take a quick road test and get a license (having forgotten his), but alas the dear Inspector Bailey turned a deaf ear, saying he was too busy. Whereupon he took his little cane and went out for what appeared to be his daily walk.

So we walked the length of the town picking up a few groceries, etc., and went as we had been directed, to the Harbor Lights for lunch. We were a little shocked to learn from our bill that two pieces of pie were $1.30 and a little dab of ice cream on the two pieces was $.50 extra. So henceforth we asked the price before we ordered! . . . Taxi back to Long Bay—$6.00.

Later: We walked down the road toward Smuggler's Cove, as we'd been told the beach there was the best place for swimming (it seemed the beach at Long Bay was too rocky for safety). But after I'd climbed a couple of those steep hills, I was done in. We turned back, passed the coconut plantation, and went back to the beach for a long trek, picking up a few shells and coral, and getting attacked by a few more bugs and mosquitoes. While I got supper, Jack scrambled up the mountain behind our cabin.

January 8: We went swimming in the pool before breakfast again, which I really enjoyed. After breakfast, tidying up the cottage, etc., we put some bread and cheese in our bag (and a can of ginger ale) and set out up the mountain. Jack had discovered that the Brahmin cattle, owned by the local farmer, knew the best way up, for they went by there to feed every day. So we followed their path, but I had to stop and rest about every ten yards, it was so steep and rocky. At last we reached a spot where a little bird's nest was—about two inches off the ground in a bush. Then it was only a short climb to the top, where the view of the bay on the other side was breathtaking. We found some shade, spread our blanket, and had our snack. We remained there for an hour or so. From this vantage point, we could see a small channel in the sea, down by the coconut plantation, which seemed clear of rocks, and later in the afternoon, we went swimming there and found we could indeed walk on beautiful sand as far out as we cared to go beyond the breakers. Back by the coconut grove, where we picked up a few. Some were declared no good by Zachary Stout, our farmer friend, who offered to chop away the tough outer covering with his machete. But the one that was good had deliciously sweet milk and good meat, which we kept nibbling away at.

January 9: When I woke up in the A.M. I observed that the tops of my feet were covered with a rash—the bane of my existence. I could not tell whether it was a mass of bites from the sand flies or some allergy flaring up. I had bumps all over, various sizes and degrees of itchiness, which I knew to be bites, but the feet looked a little different. Jack set off alone for the long hike to the village east of here. I sat most of the A.M. by the big open living room window, sewing, reading, and enjoying the view of the sea and the chain of islands beyond. I watched the farmer struggling to get his donkey going up the hill, first pulling, then pushing, then back to pulling again. There were donkeys, goats, chickens, and pigs all running around everywhere that there were people living. They say it is too hot and generally too dry to grow many vegetables here. Most foods are brought in from the U.S., Puerto Rico, and England it appears.

We went back for a swim in the P.M. by the coconut grove. We later gathered five more coconuts and had a leisurely walk home along the beach collecting shells, arriving about 6:00 P.M.

January 10: Though my feet were a little swollen and

115

still covered with little red bumps, they didn't feel as bad as they looked, so we set out about 10:00 A.M. for the village at Carrot Bay. The first hill was the toughest to climb, but we made it by stopping to rest several times. The going was easy down the other side, past Sebastian's, where there was a cluster of houses and huts. The road was fairly flat the rest of the way, but muddy and holey in spots. In the village were two schools, a church and perhaps thirty to forty small dwellings, all inhabited it seemed by native West Indians. At the far end an old man ambled down the road, eating some bread or a bun and did not seem averse to conversation, as many of them are—perhaps because it was so difficult for us to understand each other, though we all *do* speak English. Anyway, he was Mr. Leonard, a builder of some repute and he told us more than we had yet been able to learn about the price of land ($5,000 an acre was not unusual) and of building (a two-bedroom cottage such as the one we were living in was about $15,000).

Also, we were informed that Mr. Penrose owned Long Bay and had bought up quite a bit of land, including the top of the mountain above us, where he hoped to build a hotel. We had not seen any shops in the village (there were no signs out), but Mr. Leonard says there were three, but no stores. Just what the dividing line was between a shop and a store I didn't know. He pointed out the shops as we walked along the dirt road. Sure enough, if one looked closely, one could see a few shelves in a small room at the front of a house with a few tins of food, soda, etc. At Sebastian's some youngsters pointed out a shop and said they had chicken. "Oh, I'll buy a chicken," I said with some eagerness, as we were almost out of meat. "But they don't have whole chickens—only wings."

Nowhere can one find fresh fish, though we were

walking along the edge of a sea, which abounded in them a few feet away. At irregular intervals a truck did come around with fish, and everyone in the village came hurrying to the call of a conch shell to pay fantastic prices for it.

Back to the cottage at last, very weary, I soaked my feet in Epsom salts, as has been recommended by some nature woman and then I fell asleep while Jack painted. About 5:00 we went swimming. The sea was very rough, so much so that we couldn't really get beyond the breakers. . . .

We left the island with regret, but in more comfort, aboard an aquaplane. By that point my rash had almost disappeared (I had been informed by a local native woman that the overindulgence in the consumption of coconuts could cause such a reaction) and we could settle down to enjoy our flight home above the beautifully sunset-colored clouds. So we said good-bye to Tortola.

March 18: Went to Cape Cod via train and bus to visit Carol, Jim and Cheri.

March 30: Rich brought Stef home from New York. They announced they plan to get married next Friday.

April 3: Carol and Jim fly down from Boston. Stef's family (parents, Carol, Steve) arrive in the afternoon. All have dinner here.

April 4: The wedding, noon, the justice of the peace in Northport. All back here for lunch. Carol and Jim to McArthur Airport about 4:30.

April 9: Granny Bollam arrives Kennedy Airport at 1:40 P.M.

August 23: Again my heart is heavy. We are overworked, but Jack could never be convinced of that. Though he complains constantly of aches and pains, he finds some other excuse for it and I've no doubt that next year he will plan the same rigorous, never-ending sched-

117

ule of work. By God's blood, if there are more than eighteen beds of mums planted, I shall not put one vegetable seed in the ground!

November 6: Drove alone to Narragansett, Rhode Island. Spent the night and on the seventh brought Carol and Cheri home with me. Carol has the mumps and stays ten days.

1970

Well, here goes my "little black book." For years you have been making jokes about what I was writing in my little black book. So now I'm making it a reality!

At last I'm ready to openly admit that which my woman's intuition has been telling me for some time: that man-woman relationship called love is finished between us. We no doubt join a club, the members of which run into the millions—the poor souls who indeed live lives of quiet desperation, clinging together for the home, or the children, or to be cared for in old age—but finding little of joy and delight in life.

So I cross off that "happiness" bit. Health? I shall try my hardest. Peace? Perhaps an inner peace can be had—through one's love of one's children and the closeness to nature and its wonders. I don't expect we can ever be good companions again. We have not been, you and I, really, for a long time. It need not have been—need not have been—I kept saying. It takes so little to keep me happy—to fill me with that lovely warm feeling of contentment—a garden, some bread to bake, books to read. But most of all, someone to be kind and gentle, to walk with me arm in arm on a quiet evening. Someone who actually *wants* to go on a picnic with me and can find the time! You see, I wasn't kidding about that *one* picnic this past summer. But we never made it, did we? And I suppose it's just as well, because the few outings we have managed the last few years have been pretty miserable affairs, because you never really wanted to go. . . . The wind is rising and it appears to be raining. Tomorrow it will get quite cold—perhaps in the 20's, the forecasters say. I wonder if I should have covered the strawberries? I raked leaves until it was too dark to see. Even then the wind was strong and a lot of the leaves, which I was attempting to gather for my compost heap, were blown away. The sky was like cold steel; the clouds and tree silhouetted against it in stark black. The clouds were suddenly tinged with mauve, and then it became too dark to continue my raking.

"Poor you—with so many flowers to pick, and beset by so many ailments—from ear trouble to hemorrhoids."

You commented at supper that the doctor had assured you there were no hormones in those pills you have been taking. That you had said to him, "You'll have to get me a girl friend if I keep taking those pills." That didn't strike me as a very funny joke. But then perhaps I have lost my sense of humor.

So you want to write a book about your philosophy? That's good. I hope to God you can become interested enough in something to get you out of this horrible rut.

1975

December 19: Having thrashed about in his bed all night, Jack, about 6:00 A.M., made his often repeated inquiry, "Are you awake?" And having been asked whether I was asleep or half asleep, I *am* indeed now awake.

"It's got to be stopped," he said. I knew he was referring to Mother's trip to America, which was to take effect tomorrow.

December 21: It was snowy, windy, and cold, about 22 degrees, when I set out for a long walk about 10:30 A.M. I had to clear my brain of those morbid thoughts if I could. "Make a point of listening and observing," I told myself. There are the tracks of Mr. Nurnberger and his dog. How far up the road *do* they walk each day? This day anyway they stopped at the end of Dunlop Road.

Is there a colder spot on Long Island than the road between the two open fields beyond the Rowel farm? I doubt it. I almost met my Waterloo coming back up that hill in a snowstorm last winter. Today was not quite as bad—but bad enough. I turned up my jacket collar and held it around my neck. Walking is particularly treacherous—ice underneath the snow—so that I cannot move my legs along freely, but must take short steps and feel my way carefully.

1978

Sunday Night, January 15: I'm writing by candlelight while Jack and Cliff watch the Superbowl game (with the television hooked up to the generator). We are in the throes of the worst ice storm of everyone's memory. Trees are in shreds, and our hedges are flat on the ground.

July 4: My sister Myrtle died this A.M. (in the night). A hectic day followed, trying to get ready for the trip South and leave things here sufficiently organized for Jack's niece Veronica's arrival from England tomorrow. James, Catherine, and Ward came by and picked me up

Ghosts in the graveyard on the way to school,
long, long ago.

about 10:00 P.M. We drove all night and the morning of the 5th arrived at Perry's before noon.

October 3: It is evening on the day of my sister Brilla's funeral. She died sometime between two and three a.m. on Saturday.

I connect these events to the same year that I first became aware of a change taking place inside me and remembered it as the beginning of Parkinson's. However, I didn't go to the doctors about this for some time. Yes, 1978 was a very bad year for me.

1982

A drizzly, cold day, June 6: At the end of the rock garden, underneath the magnolia tree, was a little scilla. Upon my first venture into the garden each year for signs of spring—perhaps February or March—I would find it there, poking its blue head through the leaves that autumn winds had blown into the crevices of the rocks.

Upon sight of this little scilla, my heart leaped up, for to me it was a symbol of spring eternal, of love and life everlasting. To the bulldozer it was nothing, mangled beneath piles of rocks and dirt and chopped magnolia branches.

1983

October 6: Memories rise up out of the mists of the past. They have shapes that are not sharp and clear-cut, but emerge and recede in succession like ghosts (the ghosts I used to imagine inhabited the graveyard I walked past on they way to school). Events could have taken place at any time over a span of many years, 1920, or '25 or '29—who knows when I first became aware of these recurring events or perhaps a singly occurring one relating to my childhood and my reaching of maturity?

Spring, possibly early March. Fields everywhere are being plowed, a man following along behind a plow and a mule. I am mystified at the unerring eye of both man and mule, because the furrow is straight as a die and arrives precisely at the pole set up at the other side of this ten-acre field. If one is daring, shoes come off and oh, how heavenly feels the soft, warm, turned-up earth.

When are the seeds planted? The cotton and the corn? Mama's garden? I don't know. It is no concern of mine. Papa knows the right time, and he takes care of it. When to plow, when to plant, when to fertilize, when to hoe and when to harvest. Papa knows. In the later years when he is sometimes laid up for weeks with rheumatism, he knows each morning what work is to be done that day.

And after the seeds are sown, will it rain so that they will germinate? Papa doesn't know that. Only God knows that—sitting up there above those fluffy cottony clouds. I can sometimes imagine that I see His face or perhaps His whole body, fleetingly, as the clouds change shapes. I climb up the ladder and lie on the roof to watch them and dream that I'm an angel flying around up there from one cloud to another.

People Who Buy Flowers

A few years ago, we decided to try some retail sales after having sold only wholesale for so many years. It was a great success—too much so for our parking facilities.

And I found many women just came to talk. I found it very difficult to be rude to them in order to get on to another customer.

There is this one I shall call Anna, because I don't know her real name. She came for the first time last year, sad and distraught, was trying to get interested in something and thought planting some flowers around the house might be a beginning. Soon her story came tumbling out, with tears running down her cheeks: her husband had died of cancer several months ago, leaving her with three children. He *left* her with three children! Try as she might, she could not adjust, she just groped from day to day. She drove a Mercedes sports car, so I assumed she was not destitute. But money doesn't count, does it, Anna? I feel great pity for her.

And then there was Rose. She came in on the way home from work, passed here every day, and for so long had admired our flowers and wanted to stop but never got around to it until now. She was driving an oldish somewhat beaten-up car. She bought two mums for gifts and said she'd come again on Friday—pay day—and get one for herself. Her face was troubled. I gave her some apples and tomatoes that I'd just picked from the garden. "You see," she said, "my husband divorced me in April, and that's why I'm short of cash. Things are hard on me at the moment." She told me about her children. Her daughter was getting married soon.

"Yes, my husband divorced me after thirty years of marriage, and he's remarried already." She choked back the tears. "Why am I telling you all this, someone I never saw before! What's your name?" "Bea," I told her. "Good-bye, Bea." "Good-bye, Rose."

Immediately afterward another car came in. She had been here before, said my husband told her I made a delicious apple pie. She was chubby and bouncy, picked out a couple of pots, bang, bang, said they were beautiful—she just loved flowers, loved kids, loved all living things. "Life is so fragile. I love life; my father died when I was nine. I'm fifty-one and have been a widow twice."

Once a customer came in and remarked, "There is an aura of peace about this place that one can feel as soon as one enters the driveway." That remark gave me more encouragement than I had received in some time.

1985

October: At first I thought it was a squirrel—that bit of squashed flesh and fur by the side of the road where I take my daily walk. Upon closer examination I could see it was a rabbit—had been a rabbit—here's a smashed Bud can, bits of paper, a discarded Roy Rogers paper cup—large size, a paper napkin with catsup on it, and half hidden in the weeds, a large plastic Dr. Pepper bottle. Litter, litter everywhere, even a large paper lime bag, surely brought here for disposal, not carelessly thrown out a car window. What small minds such people have!

But wait! Among all these "uglies" must be something beautiful. Nature won't be outdone. There are Queen Ann's lace, blue Campion, white trumpetlike flowers on a vine and scads of goldenrod, in fact on my return trip on the other side of the road, a field full of beautiful yellow goldenrod. I even spied the seed head, soft and fluffy, of a dandelion, seeds not yet blown by the wind to their resting place to await spring.

There on the road is a lone red and yellow maple leaf. Along the railroad tracks are a number of sumacs, already displaying their autumn reds.

VI

Facing the Challenge

After I'd finished reading Keith Mano's *Bert & Me* (*Modern Maturity,* March-April, 1999), I handed the magazine to my husband and said, "Read this. It's the most positive thing I've read yet on Parkinson's Disease. Mano takes it as lightly and humorously as possible, which leaves one less bitter and more accepting of a challenging situation." Well, I can't top that, but here's my own account.

I have Parkinson's Disease; a plain statement to which one might add "pure and simple." But PD is neither pure nor simple; it is devious, unpredictable, and unrelenting. Sometimes it is merciful in that it can take several years to reach its fullest impact upon our lives, but sooner or later Parky (the nickname I have given to my PD) will do its "thing." And if we don't fight to win, it will win all the battles and the war for sure.

About twenty years ago, the first indication that something wasn't quite normal was that something was different about my entire left side. I felt this only when I lay down at night, a vague feeling that my left side detached itself from the right. I went to our family doctor, Dr. Sainsbury, and he referred me to a neurologist, no one in particular. I called a medical group on East Main Street in Huntington, Long Island, and was given an appointment with Dr. Robinson. After examining me in the manner of all neurologists looking for clues, he sent me to the lab for a CAT scan. When the results showed up negative on all other counts, he diagnosed my Parkinson's disease.

I remained perfectly calm and unruffled. I felt well and, as far as I could observe, I was in good health. I vaguely remembered a cousin whose husband had PD, and I remember having felt sorry for him because of his inability to walk without a shuffle. But my gait was perfectly normal. I would follow every health rule in my daily living, carry on as I had been and not let this bugaboo get the better of me. I made no effort to learn more about the disease; I didn't read about it or think about it.

Within a few weeks, my husband and I learned that our good friend, Henry Butcher, had also been diagnosed with PD. We had both been through some traumatic experiences during that year: Henry and Arline had lost the younger of their two daughters in a car accident; I had lost two sisters and a third had almost died from a heart by-pass. I wondered at the time if those losses could have had any part in bringing on PD. I'm still wondering. But Parky doesn't let anybody in on its secrets.

Dr. Robinson put me on Sinemet at once, though at this time I had hardly any indication of my illness. I rather think it's a mistake to start a patient on Sinemet until it's really needed because the sooner started the sooner side effects, dyskinesia (involuntary movements) in particular, show up.

Things continued in this manner for several years. Dr. Robinson had me go in to be tested once or twice a year. He would examine me, renew my prescriptions, and say, "Come back in about six months or a year." In the meantime I followed all the health rules, walked two to three miles a day, vacationed with my husband in the winters and with our children in the summers. During the summer vacations, I would hike with the rest of them, in upstate New York, Maine, and Nantucket, with no problems. I continued to work in the nursery when I had any time to spare, giving little thought to my illness.

After about ten or twelve years, I began to notice differences. I would fall occasionally and became aware of slight dyskinesia. Dr. Robinson noticed it too and added other medication to the Sinemet. It began with Amantadine and Xanax, I believe. I hadn't started a daily record at that time.

After that I tried practically every new drug that came on the market, but nothing had much effect on the inexorable, forward march of Parky. Step by step it took possession of my movements, indeed, my life. I found myself reading everything I could find on the subject of Parkinson's disease, and my thoughts were constantly on how I could outsmart this "thing," by coping with every new handicap that befell me. I resisted the cane and wheelchair as long as possible (Now I use the cane when I'm in a really bad "off" period). And I have consented to use a walker with four wheels, with two front ones that swivel. This gives me support and more confidence in my walking agility . . . for I haven't given up my daily walk. It has been shortened, but still I keep it up.

I believe it was sometime during 1994 that a rumor spread that Dr. Robinson was closing his Huntington office and would be operating out of his Glen Cove office only. My husband was always there with me, and we, who like to have our doctor close at hand, made an appointment with another doctor at the Huntington Neurological Associates. At that time I had only a slight walking problem and little dyskinesia. After a cursory examination, he said I didn't have Parkinson's and took me off all medications. The first day everything went O.K., but the second day was a disaster. Needless to say, I went back on my medication as soon as possible. (But things have never been the same since. Despite this, through sheer determination, I do everything I can to keep going and to fight Parky with every weapon I have).

When this doctor instructed his secretary not to give me another appointment, I knew he didn't want me for a patient, but he was kind enough to suggest I call Stonybrook Hospital and North Shore University Hospital and he was sure I could find a suitable doctor at one of them. We called and decided on Stonybrook simply because it was easier and quicker to get to. We made an appointment with Dr. Oded Gerber. We found him quite satisfactory and it was he who, after having me as his patient and observing that my dyskinesia was getting worse, first mentioned the word "Pallidotomy." I had read about it but never given it much thought. But now I began to take it seriously and read everything I could get my hands on about it. We made a decision to "Go for it!" We chose NYU Medical Center.

Once the ball started rolling, there was no stopping it. We soon discovered, however, that it wasn't a matter of just picking a surgeon and hospital. We learned that I had to be tested by at least five neurological specialists. I had CAT, MRI, and PET scans, and cognition and balance tests. Also, I had to have a complete physical. Any one of these doctors could have said they didn't consider me a good candidate and the whole thing would have been off. Also, the NYU doctors were generally reluctant to perform this surgery on anyone over 65, and I was 80 at that time. But all my tests came off "with flying colors," they said. Then Anne O'Sullivan, the nurse who helped coordinate things, asked me if I was superstitious, to which I replied I definitely was not. "Well, you're coming up. You're scheduled for Friday the thirteenth, September 1996."

September 15, 1996

I was discharged from the Hospital for Joint Diseases today (in New York City), having had a pallidotomy on Friday, the 13th. Dr. Alterman performed the surgery. It's difficult to be objective about it because it was the worst experience of my life. To have my head put in a frame at 7:00 A.M., stapled and bolted down for approximately three hours during which time I had to stay awake to be responsive when asked questions or directed to perform certain movements, to hear the probe being made into my brain, to hear the static when the probe touched an active area, then to hear the lesions being made and asked to perform certain responses between the "snipping" of each laser-cut lesion, all made for an unforgettable experience. Then, after my head was taken out of the frame, I felt such blessed relief, gave the V-sign to the doctors, and told them a joke about huggers and muggers.

However, I was then told that I had to go for a CAT scan, there to have another long wait in the hallway. I guess it was around noon when I was finally able to see Jack, and Rich and Stef. I was then taken to the ICU. My first thoughts upon being told it was over were, "I'm alive! I can see! I can talk!"

Today

I don't know about today. If you asked me if the operation did any good, I'd have to say, I don't really know. It did what Dr. Alterman promised for sure; it helped the dyskinesia on the left side. You go into it thinking, "Maybe—just maybe—you will start getting better instead of heading down that slippery slope with nothing to stop you." But for my husband, the rest of the family, and my friends, I might have given up long ago. But they say differently. They say I'm a fighter and would never give up. That gives me courage.

I continue my daily walks, though my family doesn't like me to go alone anymore. I have found several tree branches with forks in them at various heights, and I take them (with thanks to Yogi Berra who said, "When you come to a fork in the road, take it."). I swing on those branches. I also use our double clothesline, and with Jane Fonda's workout tape, I can do a dance with my feet that bears a slight resemblance to the Highland fling.

Since I did not feel up to actually walking in the Parkinson's Unity Walk (an annual fundraiser in New York City), I came up with the idea of selling blackberries at our 72 Dunlop Road residence. We had an overabundance of them in our garden, and I thought maybe I could start my own fund instead. I soon found I could sell all we had and more had that been the case. And after they were finished, I found I had made the grand total of $353, which was submitted to the Parkinson's Research Fund.

Operation Blackberry gave us some memorable moments and prompted my husband to remark that courage in the face of apparently insurmountable odds is the true mark of bravery, and it's better to laugh than it is to cry.

Epilogue

I have been away from the South for a number of years now, and away from Sampson County, except for an occasional visit, for sixteen years. My last visit was several years ago, and such a change had been wrought, I hardly recognized my neighborhood. A big new highway had replaced the old winding dirt road, whose ruts had been cut more by wagons going to the cotton gin than by cars. Electric wires crisscrossed the countryside, and my oldest sister Lillian once told me, "I wouldn't swap my electric washer for a brand new car."

Since that last visit, my old home too has been wired, and there's a new fridge and a new gas stove, which would add confusion to bewilderment should I go back.

This is progress, and I support today's progress with all my might and main, especially in the South. But sometimes in the spring, wherever I happen to be, a soft, balmy breeze, which seems to come straight from North Carolina, brushes against my cheek and stirs sweet memories of an easy, less progressive South. Then I long very much to go back and find it just as it was when each spring, as a little girl, I ran along newly plowed rows to feel the coolness of the earth on my bare feet, picked wild violets by the handful on the Big Ditch bank, sought out every little spring and tiny waterfall in the pasture stream, and waded up to my knees chasing minnows.

Time Line

Katherine Beatrice Lockerman—born June 29, 1916—Salemburg, North Carolina.

1923—Attended Corinth School, Salemburg, North Carolina.

1924–1930—Attended Salemburg Grammar School.

1931–1934—Attended Salemburg High School.

1934–1939—Attended Berry College, Rome, Georgia—B.S. in English Literature.

1939—Attended U.N.C. at Chapel Hill, summer school.

1939–1941—Taught sixth grade music—Baron DeKalb School Westville, South Carolina.

1941—Attended University of Tenn. at Knoxville, summer school.

1941–1942—Employed as cryptographer by F.B.I., Washington D.C.

1942—Married Owen Jack Bollam, September 2.

1942–1943—Resided in Truro, Nova Scotia, Canada.

1943–1944—Resided in Charlottetown, P.E.I. Canada—Richard Owen born February 29, 1944.

1944–1945—Resided in Goderich, Ontario, Canada.

1945—Salemburg (January to February). Truro (February to May)—Harrogate, England (May to June).

1945–1946—Resided in Hillside, Bury, Sussex, England.

1946—Resided in Smithtown, New York, Cornell Avenue (two weeks) then Hauppauge Road.

1948–2001—Resided in Huntington, New York, 72 Dunlop Road. Carol Bee born February 21, 1948.

2001–present—Residing in Wrentham, Massachusetts.